RAYMOND & GRAHAM

COOL
CAMPERS

BY Mike Knudson

ILLUSTRATED BY Stacy Curtis

VIKING

An Imprint of Penguin Group (USA) Inc.

VIKING
Published by Penguin Group
Penguin Young Readers Group, 345 Hudson Street, New York, New York 10014, U.S.A.
Penguin Group (Canada), 90 Eglinton Avenue East, Suite 700, Toronto, Ontario, Canada M4P 2Y3
(a division of Pearson Penguin Canada Inc.)
Penguin Books Ltd, 80 Strand, London WC2R 0RL, England
Penguin Ireland, 25 St Stephen's Green, Dublin 2, Ireland (a division of Penguin Books Ltd)
Penguin Group (Australia), 250 Camberwell Road, Camberwell, Victoria 3124, Australia
(a division of Pearson Australia Group Pty Ltd)
Penguin Books India Pvt Ltd, 11 Community Centre, Panchsheel Park, New Delhi – 110 017, India
Penguin Group (NZ), 67 Apollo Drive, Rosedale, North Shore 0632, New Zealand
(a division of Pearson New Zealand Ltd.)
Penguin Books (South Africa) (Pty) Ltd, 24 Sturdee Avenue, Rosebank, Johannesburg 2196, South Africa

Penguin Books Ltd, Registered Offices: 80 Strand, London WC2R 0RL, England

First published in 2010 by Viking, a division of Penguin Young Readers Group

1   3   5   7   9   10   8   6   4   2

Text copyright © Mike Knudson, 2010
Illustrations copyright © Stacy Curtis, 2010
All rights reserved

LIBRARY OF CONGRESS CATALOGING-IN-PUBLICATION DATA
Knudson, Mike.
Raymond and Graham, cool campers / by Mike Knudson ; illustrated by Stacy Curtis.
p. cm.
Summary: Best friends Raymond and Graham decide to reinvent
themselves when they go to Camp Grizzly over the summer.
ISBN 978-0-670-01206-0 (hardcover)
[1. Camps—Fiction. 2. Popularity—Fiction. 3. Best friends—Fiction. 4. Friendship—Fiction.] I. Curtis, Stacy, ill.
II. Title. III. Title: Cool campers.
PZ7.K7836Rao 2010
[Fic]—dc22
2009024899

Manufactured in China   Set in Chaparral Pro   Book design by Jim Hoover

To Randy Evans and David Cope,
two cool campers!
—M.K.

For Michael, Mason, and Shana
—S.C.

Prologue

THE FINAL BELL rang, and the school year was officially over. We grabbed our backpacks, said good-bye to Mrs. Gibson, and ran for the front doors. Summer was here! The air smelled more like summer than it had even an hour ago at recess. I couldn't wait for sleepovers, staying up late, and best of all . . . SUMMER CAMP.

1

Party Time?

IT WAS MONDAY afternoon. School had ended over a week ago. I heard the doorbell and ran down the stairs. I knew it was my best friend, Graham. I jumped down the last three stairs only to find my sister already opening the door.

"Why hello, Geri," I heard Graham say from the front porch. "It's so lovely to see you."

"Oh, it's you," she said in her you're-even-dorkier-than-my-brother voice. And without another word she turned and walked away.

"Have a nice day," Graham called after her, with a big smile stretched across his freckly face. He was always saying stuff like that to my sister.

"How come you're so nice to her?" I asked. "She's

just as mean to you as she is to me. She thinks we're both dorks."

"Yeah, but I think she's been nicer to me lately. She probably thinks I'm cool now."

I looked down at Graham, who was much smaller than me. His legs were whiter than his socks, and his T-shirt was tucked into the front of his underpants. "I'm not so sure about that," I said.

"Well, she's still an older lady." Graham smiled. "And she's pretty cute."

A shiver went down my spine. "*Geri?* Are you serious? First of all, she's no lady. She's just my mean thirteen-year-old sister. Second of all, have you ever heard her burp? There's definitely nothing ladylike about that! And thirdly . . . don't ever say she's cute. That's just plain sick."

"Okay, okay, don't have a heart attack," Graham said, shaking his head.

We went up to my room and took turns shooting my little foam ball through the plastic rim on the back of my door. "So what should we do tonight? We need to celebrate," Graham said.

"I know. This is going to be the best week ever!"

The next day we were going to Camp Grizzly for four days. We had been looking forward to this forever. "Finally, we get to go to the real Camp Grizzly instead of Grizzly Cub camp." Grizzly Cub camp was always in August, but the camp for bigger kids was at the very beginning of the summer. It was so much cooler to be leaving right after school ended instead of having to wait.

Graham smiled and moved his eyebrows up and down. "I heard we get to have a marshmallow roast with the girls from Camp Wildflower. Diane told me that Kelly is going to camp this year too."

Graham had liked Kelly since the first grade, back when all of us boys thought girls had cooties and all the girls thought boys were gross. It was weird. I kind of liked Heidi, another girl in our class, but I would never have told her. Graham didn't care if people knew how he felt about Kelly. And even though she didn't like him back, he didn't mind. He just kept liking her anyway.

"Well, we should definitely do something fun tonight, since it's our last night at home for the rest of the week," I said.

Graham's face lit up. "Let's have a party! We can invite people over and play hide-and-seek outside."

"Great idea!" We hadn't really played any games with the neighborhood gang since school ended. Graham lived next door to Heidi, and Diane's house was on the other side of Graham's back-yard fence. A lot of our other friends lived within a block or two. I lived about two blocks up the road from Graham, but I always wished I could live next door to him.

We called a few people, but only Zach answered, and he was busy. We decided to walk over to Diane's house, and we found her and Heidi jumping on Diane's trampoline.

"Hey, can we jump with you guys?" Graham asked. He already had his shoes off and was on the trampoline. Diane jumped really high and landed next to him. He fell onto his stomach. She and Heidi kept jumping, making it impossible for him to stand up.

"What's this all about?" Diane said. "You ask if you can jump, and before we even answer you just climb right on."

"Yeah, where are your trampoline manners?" Heidi added, laughing.

"May we please jump with you?" I asked. My shoes were still on.

"Why yes, you may," Diane answered politely. I kicked off my sneakers and climbed up.

After bouncing around for a while we all lay down on the trampoline to rest.

"Hey, we were thinking of getting everyone together tonight for a party. Maybe we can play hide-and-seek or capture the flag. Do you guys want to come?" I asked.

"Tonight? We're going to Eden's birthday party," Diane said. "This summer is going to be filled with parties. Tonight it's Eden's, then next Saturday is Brad's pool party."

Graham and I looked at each other. "What pool party?"

There was a big pause, and then Heidi said, "Oh, it's nothing." I could tell by the way she looked at us that she was lying, like she felt sorry for us. "I think it's only for a few people—"

"You guys weren't invited?" Diane interrupted.

"Everyone's going. I know for a fact that Luke, Matt, and Kelly will be there. Even Lizzy." Heidi jabbed Diane in the ribs. "Oh, I mean, just a few of us."

But it was too late—we'd heard her loud and clear.

Now the confused look on Graham's face turned to anger. "You're saying that everyone was invited to a pool party at Brad's except us?"

The girls didn't know what to say, so we just sat there for a minute or two in silence.

"Even Lizzy?" I asked. Lizzy was the most annoying person in the world. She was the biggest teacher's pet, and she was so snooty she drove me nuts. I shook my head in disbelief.

"Don't worry about it. I'm sure it won't be fun," Heidi said.

Graham and I didn't feel like jumping anymore after that, so we climbed off the trampoline and walked over to Graham's house. We sat down in his front yard.

"I just can't believe this, Raymond. Did you know we were so unpopular?"

"No way. I mean, I know David kind of picks on me, and Lizzy and I have been enemies for-ever. And sure, my sister thinks we're dorks, but I always just thought that's the way sisters are. I didn't know everyone else agreed with her."

Graham lay down in the grass and looked up into the sky. "So this is what it all comes down to. We're just two dorks who are so unpopular we can't even get invited to a party that Lizzy got in-vited to. Even Matt Lindenheimer is going."

"Yeah, I always thought we were more popular than Matt—except last summer at Grizzly Cub camp. Remember how everyone thought he was so funny?"

Graham sat up. "You're right. Somehow Matt went from being plain old regular Matt to being the coolest kid at camp. But when camp was over, everything went back to normal, and he was the same old Matt 'The Brain' Lindenheimer again."

"Yeah, but now he gets invited to parties," I said. "Now he's Matt 'The Party Brain' Linden-heimer." Graham nodded in agreement. We sat there quietly and felt sorry for ourselves. Then suddenly Graham stood up.

"That's it! At school Matt's just the smart kid who always sits in the front row. Then at camp he was suddenly Mr. Popular. It's like no one knew who he really was."

"Yeah, so what?" I said.

"Well, no one really knows who *we* are at camp either," Graham said, rubbing his chin as he thought. "I say this year *we* become the Mr. Populars at camp."

"You're right," I said. "That's the best thing about camp. You can be anyone you want to be. It doesn't matter how dorky you are in real life." We both smiled.

"Who cares about the stupid party?" Graham said. "Tomorrow we'll be the most popular kids at Camp Grizzly. And who knows? Maybe the coolness will stick when we come home."

We high-fived. This was one of Graham's best ideas yet.

2

Cabin Sweet Cabin

THAT NIGHT MY mom and I packed all of my stuff. She wrote my name on the tag of my underwear with a black marker. I have no idea why she does that. I mean, of all the pieces of clothing that you could lose, why are moms so worried about underwear? I've lost a lot of jackets and sweatshirts because I take them off when I'm hot and then I forget about them. But how could you ever lose your underwear?

Everything fit into one big blue duffle bag. I was also bringing my backpack from school. It was packed with some snacks and a drink.

I could hardly sleep. I felt like my entire life was going to change the next day. When Tuesday morning finally came, I jumped out of bed, put on my shorts and T-shirt, and ran into the kitchen. No matter what time I got up, my mom always seemed to be in the kitchen making breakfast.

"Good morning, sweetie," she said. "Just in time." She set a plate piled high with French toast in the center of the table. I sat down in my usual spot and stuck my fork in the pile, pulling off about half of the toast.

Just then Dad walked in. He gave me a gentle pat on the head with the newspaper. "Whoa, slow down, big fella. Save some for your old man."

"Oh, let him eat," Mom said. "Who knows what they'll be feeding him at camp."

Dad grabbed a piece of French toast from my plate and put it on his. "He'll be fine. I'm sure they'll be eating bear steaks, squirrel stew, and other good camp food."

A terrible image of Graham and me sitting around the campfire roasting a squirrel on a stick filled my mind. I suddenly thought maybe I should eat as much as I could before leaving.

After breakfast Dad gave me a hug and told me

to be good. He also pulled out his wallet and gave me a five-dollar bill. "Here's something extra for a treat," he said. Then he left for work.

"Go tell your sister good-bye," Mom ordered. I ran up the stairs. Geri was still asleep, and I really didn't want to wake her up. She's not too pleasant in the morning. But I took a deep breath and opened the door.

"Um . . . good-bye, Geri. I'm leaving for camp." Without waiting for her to answer, I turned to leave. But Mom had come up the stairs and was standing right behind me.

"Geri, wake up and tell your brother good-bye." Mom carefully put her hand on my sister's shoulder and gave it a little nudge. Then we both stepped back quickly. Waking Geri up is like playing with a bomb. If you don't do it just right, she'll explode.

"Go away!" She rolled over and pulled her pillow over her head.

"You're not going to see Raymond until Saturday. Don't you want to say good-bye?" Mom said. Geri let out an awful groan and sat up. Her hair was in a big snarly mess. I took another step back.

"Fine!" she said, putting on her biggest fake smile. "Good-bye, Raymond. I will miss you so much. What will I ever do without you?" Then she collapsed back onto her bed and pulled the covers over her head.

"See, she's going to miss you," Mom said with a smile. I wasn't too sure about that.

We loaded my bag into the car and headed over to Graham's house. We pulled into his driveway and honked. My mom got out and chatted with his mom while we put his bag in the trunk with mine.

"This is going to be so awesome!" Graham said. "You should see how much candy I brought."

"Cool, I've got a bunch too. Hey, what's that smell?" I sniffed around closer to Graham.

"It's probably either the sunscreen or the bug spray, or maybe a combination of the two," Graham said. "My mom covered me in both. She said the sun is stronger in the mountains and the mosquitoes are everywhere."

I plugged my nose. "I think the smell will scare

away all of the mosquitoes." The sunscreen was probably a good idea. Graham has a million freckles, and when he gets sunburn they turn green. I think it's cool, but he doesn't like it. We climbed into the backseat, and then we were officially on our way to camp.

"I've been thinking about the coolness situation," I said. "Last year, part of Matt's coolness was the cub pack he was in. Most of the kids in his group were pretty cool. Plus, his leader was the best. So whatever happens, we need to get into the best group."

"Yeah, you're right," Graham said. "But the problem is they just assign you to your group. We can't do anything about it. What if you and I don't even get in the same group?" He was right. I guess we would just have to hope for the best. We tried to think of some other things we could do to be really cool, but we couldn't think of much.

"I know," Graham said. "We need to say funny things. I don't know how Matt got so funny, but he was a crazy man at camp."

I agreed. "Okay, what should we say that's funny?" We thought for a while but couldn't come up with anything.

Graham shrugged his shoulders. "I'm sure we will think of funny things when we need to." I hoped he was right.

The rest of the ride up we played every car ride game we could think of. You know, like the license plate game where you try to find the most different states, or the alphabet game where you try to find every letter from *A* to *Z* on billboards and signs. And finally, we played ninety-nine bottles of pop on the wall. My mom made us stop after we counted down to forty-seven bottles. She said it was a fun song, but it was driving her crazy. I could tell from her voice that she meant it. But I didn't mind, because just as we stopped singing we passed a sign that read CAMP GRIZZLY NEXT RIGHT.

We turned under a giant arch made of logs. On the side of the road there was a big grizzly bear carved out of wood, and it was holding a sign that read CAMP GRIZZLY STRAIGHT AHEAD. Graham and I bounced up and down in our seats.

"We're here! We're here!" we shouted together.

"There's the lake." Graham pointed.

"Wow, it looks even bigger than last year!" I said. "And there's Camp Wildflower way over there." Camp Wildflower was the girls' camp. Heidi, Diane, and a bunch of girls from our school go there every summer.

We pulled into the dusty parking lot, where some friendly camp people directed us to a free space. One thing I like about camp is that everyone is always so happy to be there.

Mom walked us up to the lodge to check in. A guy in a yellow Camp Grizzly T-shirt was sitting at a table. Mom told him who we were, and he thumbed down a list and put a check mark by each of our names. Then he gave us name tags, a map, and a list of rules. He also handed us each a card with our name and cabin number on it.

"Sweet, we're both in cabin five!" I high-fived Graham.

The guy told us to take our things to the cabin and then go to the mess hall for lunch when we heard someone ring the big gong in the middle of camp. After lunch, we had to be back at the lodge at two o'clock for the opening ceremonies.

"Say something funny," Graham whispered to me. I tried, but wasn't feeling very funny.

"Aye aye, captain," Graham said, saluting the camp guy and squinting one eye like a pirate.

He gave Graham an odd look. "Um, okay."

Graham turned to me and gave me a thumbs-up sign. The whole pirate saluting thing must have been Graham's joke.

"Should we go find your cabin?" Mom asked.

"We can find it on our own," I said. I didn't think walking around camp with Mom would look too cool. "I think girls and moms aren't allowed. I'll see you on Saturday." I gave her a quick hug.

"Not so fast, sweetie." She pulled me in and gave me a humongous hug. Not only that, but she gave me a kiss on the forehead.

"Have fun, and be extra careful," she said.

"I will." She had already told me to be careful like twelve times that day.

"And don't lose your underwear. I wrote your name in—"

"Shh!" I interrupted. "I know, I know. My name's on the tag," I whispered. Graham was giggling.

My mom finally figured out that she was embarrassing me. She gave me one last hug. "I'll see you bright and early on Saturday morning. Have fun! I love you," she said.

"Me too," I said quickly.

"Me too what?" she asked. I knew she'd understood what I meant. Why can't she just know that I love her even when I just say "me too"? I mean, she's my mom. Of course I love her. It's like the law.

"I love you too," I said. She grinned and walked away. Finally, Graham and I lugged our bags to cabin five. There was camp staff all along the path to show us where to go. The last person pointed to our cabin. It was made of big logs. Three wooden steps led to a small porch and an old, scratched-up wooden door with a number five nailed to it.

"Now remember, we need to be funny," Graham said.

"Right, I'll try."

Graham pushed the door open. "Ah, home sweet home."

"Don't you mean 'cabin sweet cabin'?" I said, practicing at being funny.

Inside, we were met by a loud, "Shhh." It came from a small kid by the window. He was even smaller than Graham, and he was hovering over a jar. There was another jar nearby.

We dropped our bags and went over.

"Hey, what's in the jars?" Graham said, reaching for one of them.

The kid shielded the jars from Graham with his body. "Shhh," he repeated.

"Sorry," Graham whispered. I stretched my neck around the kid to get a glimpse.

"I think he's about to make a cocoon," the kid said.

I stretched my neck more but still couldn't see. "Who's making a cocoon?"

The kid huddled around his jars until he finally decided we were no longer threats. Then he slowly stepped back to let us see. "Jeremiah," he said.

"Who's Jeremiah?" Graham asked. He slowly stuck his face up to the jar. "Hey, it's a caterpillar."

I put my face up next to Graham's. "Jeremiah's a caterpillar?" Graham and I looked at each other. "That's a pretty big name for a bug." I chuckled, trying to be funny.

The kid looked a little offended. "Hey, caterpillars are people too. Everyone deserves a name."

"Sorry," I said. "I didn't mean that he didn't deserve a . . . hey, did you say that caterpillars are people?"

"Of course. He's alive, isn't he?" he shot back. He was pretty feisty for a little guy. As I stood there trying to figure out how bugs are people, Graham piped in.

"By the way, I'm Graham," he said, pointing to his name tag.

The kid reached out to shake Graham's hand. His name tag said ANDY. "I'm Andy, but everyone calls me BB, for Bug Boy. In case you haven't noticed, I like bugs." I introduced myself too. BB told us that he liked to find and keep bugs in his room at home. His mom had made him let them all go before he came to camp so she wouldn't have to take care of them. So he brought some of his empty jars to find bugs here. He'd found the caterpillar on a leaf right outside of our cabin.

I looked around the room. There was a set of bunk beds on the wall by the window and another against the opposite wall. I could see that BB had already claimed the lower bunk bed by the window.

"Do you want the top bunk or the bottom?" Graham asked. Since I got stuck with the bottom last year, I thought I'd take the top. Unfortunately, without waiting for my answer, Graham climbed up to the top and made himself at home.

"I guess I'll take the bottom," I sighed. I could have probably taken the other top bunk, but I still didn't know BB very well, and I thought I'd better stay on Graham's side of the room.

Just then the door opened and a huge figure walked in. The light from outside made it hard to see his face. I thought he must have been one of the camp directors or some other adult.

"Hello, fellow cabinmates," said the large shadow in a jolly voice. As the door closed and

the outside light dimmed, his face came into full view. He wasn't a man at all. He was just the biggest kid I had ever seen. Not only was he tall but he was big all over. His legs looked like they were as thick as my whole body. BB, Graham, and I stared in amazement.

"Hi," BB finally said. He looked up at our enormous roommate and held up his hand. "My name's Andy, but you can call me BB."

"Nice to meet you, BB. My name is Paul, but everyone just calls me Tiny."

Tiny? I thought. There was nothing tiny about him. Then I figured that must be why they called him Tiny. You know, like when a bald guy is nicknamed Curly.

"Hey, I'll bet I know why they call you Tiny," I said, trying to be funny again.

"You do?" Tiny answered. He looked confused, like he wondered how I could possibly know. In fact, he looked so confused that I suddenly felt like maybe I shouldn't say what I was thinking.

"So why do you think they call me Tiny?" he

asked. I couldn't say, "Because you're huge" if that really wasn't the reason. Maybe he didn't even know he was huge.

"Um . . . why don't you tell me why, and I'll tell you if I was right," I said. His confused look turned to a friendly smile, and he happily told us his story.

"Well, when I was born, I came two months early and weighed about five pounds. I was so small I had to stay in the hospital for over three weeks. We have a picture of me, and I was just a little bigger than my dad's hands. The doctor said I was a miracle baby. Since then, my dad and everyone else have called me Tiny. So why did you think they called me Tiny?" The guys turned to me and waited for my answer.

I began to sweat. "That's exactly what I was thinking," I said. "Only I was going to say that you weighed four pounds, not five."

"Wow," Tiny said. "You're good."

3

Weenie and Freckles

IT WAS NOT long before all of us felt like friends. We opened our backpacks and shared our candy with each other. Tiny had brought twice as much as the rest of us. BB had all kinds of gummy worms and other candy bugs. He told us more about all the bugs he'd collected, Tiny talked about how he liked to draw pictures, I gave a replay of the final inning of the championship baseball game we'd won a few weeks earlier, and Graham went on and on about Kelly and how beautiful she was.

"You like girls?" BB asked, scrunching up his nose. "All the girls at my school have germs."

I looked at BB and thought about all the bugs he found and dug for in the dirt. I wouldn't think germs would bother a guy like him.

Graham put one hand on BB's shoulder. "Kelly's no ordinary girl. She's like . . . um . . . help me out, Raymond. Tell them how amazing Kelly is." Our two new friends turned to me, awaiting my incredible description of Kelly. I didn't know what to say. She just seemed like any other girl to me. But I knew I had to help Graham.

"Let's see," I started. I thought back to the Valentine's Day boxes we decorated in school last February. "To begin with, she can cut perfect hearts out of pink paper. And then there's how . . . um . . ." Graham stared at me with wide eyes as I tried to describe the girl he'd admired his entire life. "Well . . . there's . . . um . . . oh yeah, those great glasses she wears," I continued. Graham smiled and nodded. I couldn't think of anything else. Somehow, even though I had known Kelly since the first grade, it all came down to cutting out paper hearts and wearing glasses.

They all stared, waiting for more. Unfortunately, that was it.

"That's about it," I said.

"Yes, she's perfect." Graham sighed. BB and Tiny looked at each other and shrugged their shoulders. Just then, we heard the gong ring.

"Let's go grab some lunch," I said.

"Let me just clean my glasses first," BB said. He sat on his bed and dug through his backpack until he found a small square cloth. BB had big black-framed glasses, and when he took them off his eyes looked small and squinty. As he cleaned his glasses, Tiny carefully moved over to the bugs in their jars.

"These bugs can't get out, can they?" he asked. He sounded nervous.

"Nope, they're safe in there," BB answered, squinting at Tiny.

Tiny looked from one jar to the next. "What are you going to put in this empty one?" He unscrewed the lid of the empty jar and held it up. BB put his glasses back on.

"What empty one?" He looked up, gasped, then leaped from his bed and grabbed the jar out of Tiny's hand. "Where's Harry?" he screamed.

Tiny dropped the lid and shook his hands. "Who's Harry?"

"He was probably hiding on the lid!" BB shouted. He picked up the lid and examined it. "Oh no, he must have jumped off when you opened the jar." The seriousness of BB's voice made us all scared.

"Who's Harry?" we all asked together.

"He's the big, hairy brown spider I found under the front steps of the cabin. I was still trying to figure out what kind of spider he was."

Graham and I immediately jumped to Graham's top bunk.

Tiny had a look of terror on his face. "Aaaah, I hate spiders!" he screamed. It was a high-pitched scream that you wouldn't expect from a big guy like him. He was turning in circles and waving his hands in the air.

"Wait! Stop!" BB yelled. Tiny froze with his

back toward us. BB crept slowly toward Tiny. "Don't move."

"Why?" Tiny cried. Then Graham and I both realized what BB was doing. Graham pointed to Tiny's back.

"It's on your back! Harry's on your back!"

"What?" Tiny let out the most terrible, piercing shriek I'd ever heard. He started jumping around like a maniac, kicking his feet and swinging his arms in all directions. He looked like a crazed karate master. He ripped his shirt off and threw it on the floor. Then he leaped over to the corner of the room and stood there shaking.

BB bent down and carefully lifted the shirt. The spider was still there. Slowly, he moved the shirt to the opening of the jar. After a quick tap to the back of the shirt, Harry was back in his jar.

We all took a deep breath. I looked at Tiny and wondered how a big guy like him could jump around like that. BB handed him his shirt.

Tiny examined it thoroughly and pulled it over his head. Then he gave one last big shiver. He took

a few deep breaths to calm himself down. "I'm okay," he said. "Sorry, I don't really like spiders."

"Really?" Graham said. "We couldn't tell." Then we all started laughing. BB put the jar back on the table, and we walked down to the mess hall.

The room was filled with long tables. At one end, there was a huge fireplace that I could probably stand up in, and at the other end were two long serving tables. Four staff members were serving the food. A few kids were already sitting down and eating, but no one was in line, so we walked right up.

The choices were hot dogs or hamburgers. There were also chips, bananas, cookies, and cartons of milk. I chose a hot dog, Graham and BB both picked burgers, and Tiny took one of each.

"Where should we sit?" Graham asked, scanning all of the empty tables. I set my tray down on the table right in front of us.

Graham placed his tray next to mine, and Tiny and BB sat across the table from us. Tiny picked up his hot dog with one hand and his hamburger with the other. Then he went back and forth taking a bite out of each one.

"Wow, that's a lot of food," Graham said. "Why didn't you get a banana?"

Tiny put the hamburger down, rubbed his stomach, and made a face like he was sick. "Bananas give me gas," he said.

"Oooh," we all replied in unison. I didn't know about the rest of the guys, but I was really glad he didn't get a banana. I'm not sure why, but it seemed like gas from a huge kid like Tiny would be a lot worse than gas from a puny kid.

We sat there quietly enjoying our food until Graham broke the silence. "You know, I always wanted a nickname. You two are so lucky."

"Yeah," I agreed. "Nicknames are so cool. My sister always calls me Dork. But I don't really count that as a nickname."

Graham laughed. "Dork? That's hilarious."

"Well, she calls you Dork Junior," I shot back.

Graham's smile faded. "She does?"

"Yeah, but she thinks everyone is a dork, so it doesn't really matter." I turned back to BB and Tiny. "Does anyone even call you by your real names anymore?"

BB thought for a moment. "You know, I can't remember the last time anyone called me by my real name."

"Me neither," Tiny said. "Even my grandmother calls me Tiny."

Then it hit me. "Graham, let's get nicknames for camp."

"Yeah!" He looked at BB and Tiny. "You two can give us our nicknames."

"Why us?" BB asked. He looked a little nervous about being in charge of something so important.

"Well, we can't give ourselves nicknames," Graham said. "They have to come from someone else. Take Tiny, for example. He didn't get born one day, look in the mirror, and say, 'Wow, I am so small. I think I'll just call myself Tiny.' Someone else had to do it." I nodded in agreement.

BB and Tiny looked at each other. "Well, I guess so," Tiny said. "But I've never given anyone a nickname before. I might not be good at it."

"Don't worry," Graham said. "You'll do great."

I raised my hand. "Do mine first." I wanted

to make sure that if they could only think of one good one, I would get it.

"All right," BB said. "Let's see. It should probably be based on something you like or how you look or maybe part of your real name."

"Hmm . . ." Tiny scratched his head and looked deep into my eyes. "Tell me, Raymond, what do you really like?" At that moment I couldn't think of anything.

"I, uh, like . . . hmm, what do I like?" I looked around the room for some ideas. Then I glanced down at my tray. "Well, I like hot dogs."

"Hot dogs, huh," BB said. "How about just calling you Hot Dog?"

"Nah." I shook my head.

"How about Weenie?" Tiny said in his happy voice. "It's just another word for hot dog. You know, like—"

"No way!" I interrupted. "No one wants to be called Weenie!"

"I guess you're right," Tiny said. Graham was trying to hold back his laughter.

"Why don't you start with Graham instead?" I suggested.

Tiny turned to Graham. "Let's see. How about Red?"

"Why Red?" Graham asked.

"Because your hair is red." Tiny pointed to Graham's messy mop of curly red hair.

"Oh, yeah. Well, I don't want to be called Red. Try another."

"How about Freckles?" BB said.

"Nope. Don't like that either."

BB and Tiny both let out a heavy sigh at the same time.

"I know," BB said, sounding a little impatient. "How about 'Graham'?"

"Graham . . . hmm. I like it," Graham answered, laughing. "Let's go with that."

"And just call me Raymond," I joined in. In the end I figured being called Raymond and Graham was a lot better than being called Weenie and Freckles.

4

Toad Claws

IT WAS TWO o'clock when we finished lunch. The gong sounded again, so we all walked to the lodge together. The place was packed, and it was loud in there. Everyone was talking at the same time. I looked around for people from our school. The only ones I saw were Zach and David. They were standing next to each other across the room. I figured they must be in the same cabin. I recognized a few other kids from last year, but couldn't remember most of their names. It didn't look like Matt was there.

"Hey, isn't Matt coming?" I asked Graham.

He looked around the room. "I guess not. This will be great. One less guy trying to be popular."

The noise seemed to get louder and louder. Then, out of nowhere, the growl of a grizzly bear blared over the loudspeaker. It silenced the entire room. As we looked around, searching for the bear, the doors swung open and in ran all of the camp staff. They were cheering and clapping and jumping around like crazy.

"Let me hear you growl, Grizzlies!" one of them yelled. We all growled as loud as we could. They ran up and down the room and made their way to the big fireplace in the front of the room.

"Hello, Grizzlies!" they all called out together.

"Hello!" we all answered.

"Is that the best you've got?" one of them yelled back.

"Hello!" we screamed at the top of our lungs.

I loved this part of camp. Somehow all of the energy from the staff made me even more excited to be there. I looked over at Graham. He was jumping around and cheering. I could tell he loved this part too.

A tall guy with short hair that stuck straight

up stepped forward. "Is everyone ready for some Grizzly Fun?"

We all cheered.

"Great!" he continued. "My name is Adam, but everyone calls me Fuzzy." He rubbed his fuzzy-looking hair. We all laughed.

"I'm your camp director, and I'm excited to be part of this year's camp. And behind me is a bunch of the best Grizzly counselors on the planet." One by one the counselors stepped forward and introduced themselves.

The first one hopped forward like a frog and announced, "Howdy, Grizzlies. I'm Jeff, but you can call me Toad." He turned and hopped back in line. The other counselors followed, sharing their real names and their nicknames. They all had crazy nicknames like Flip, Gopher, and Twig. There was a big counselor who flexed his huge muscles. His nickname was Flex.

Graham leaned over to me. "I didn't hear anyone called Freckles or Weenie," he said.

"Let's hear it for the best Grizzly counselors

ever!" Fuzzy yelled. Again, more cheering. My hands were getting sore from clapping so much. Then he announced that each counselor would be assigned to three cabins, which together would make up a bear patrol. Your bear patrol would do things together all week.

I turned to Graham. "I hope we get Flex."

"Yeah, me too," Graham said. "That would be the first step toward being cool." Unfortunately, when they announced our cabin, we got Toad.

"Well, at least he's funny," I said. He actually looked kind of like a toad, especially when he hopped around.

The staff acted out some funny skits about the different activities we would be doing the rest of the week. There would be swimming, a hike, crafts, and, best of all, the big camp Olympics on the last day. And of course there was also a marshmallow roast the next night with Camp Wildflower. Fuzzy asked if anyone had any questions.

Graham elbowed me in the side. "Now's our chance, Raymond. Raise your hand and say something funny."

"What should I say? Why don't you say something?" I asked.

"Because I already did, remember?"

I looked at Graham. "You mean that pirate thing when we checked in?" I asked.

"Yeah, it was awesome. Now it's your turn." Graham raised his hand and said, "My friend Raymond has a question."

"Great, what's your question?" Fuzzy said. The room went silent. I tried to think of something funny.

"Hi, I was just wondering, what . . . um . . ."

"What were you wondering?" Fuzzy asked, trying to help me along.

"I was wondering what . . . smells in here. Yes, that's it. I was wondering what smells in here." *Perfect,* I thought. *Smells are always funny.*

Unfortunately, before anyone could appreciate my funniness, I heard David yell from across the room, "It's you that smells!" Immediately there was a roar of laughter from the crowd.

"That didn't go so well," I complained to Graham. "I just made David look more popular."

"You should have said one of those pirate things like I did," Graham said.

Fuzzy led the group in one last camp cheer, and then the meeting was over.

We all followed our counselors back to our cabins.

"Hey, Toad, can we stop at the Trading Post?" Tiny asked.

"You mean you guys haven't been to the Trading Post yet?" Toad looked completely amazed. I couldn't tell if he was joking or if he was serious. "Well, let's hop on over." He turned and hopped down the path to the Trading Post. Some of our group hopped too. I thought we looked a little silly. *This is definitely not helping us look cool*, I thought.

It appeared that most of the camp had the same idea as us. The Trading Post was packed. Most of the kids were gathered around the candy, so we went to the opposite end.

I picked up a leather string with a bear claw hanging from it. "Hey, check this out." Graham rushed over and snatched it from my hand.

"No way! A real bear claw! And it's only four ninety-nine! Nothing says cool like a real bear claw!" Suddenly, a familiar voice and a familiar punch to my arm interrupted our conversation.

"Where'd you get that plastic claw? From a plastic bear?" David laughed his crazy laugh. Life had been much happier for me since school let out, without David's nastiness and the daily slug to my arm.

"What do you mean, plastic?" Graham snapped back. "Looks pretty real to me."

"Oh sure, I know a lot of bears that have little stickers on their claws that say CHINA on them." I had learned to just ignore David, but Graham always had to have the last word.

"So you don't think there are bears in China?" Graham said.

"Even if there are, how many have stickers on their claws?" David grabbed another claw from the shelf and held it up to Graham's face. I had to agree with David, but Graham wasn't going to give up that easily.

"Have you ever examined a Chinese bear's claw up close?" Graham shot back. David just rolled his eyes and dropped the claw back on the shelf.

Just then Flex walked up. "Hey," he told David, "don't waste your time arguing with these guys over a stupid plastic claw."

Graham smiled at David. "Yeah. Take a hike."

Then I got my nerve up and added, "Yeah, take a hike up to Grizzly Peak." That was the three-mile hike we would be doing this week. I thought it was a pretty clever comment, since we were at camp.

David made a fist and punched it into his other hand. "You'd better watch what you say." Obviously, he didn't appreciate my Grizzly Peak line. Just then Toad and our patrol came over.

"What's the problem over here?" he asked.

"Are these your boys?" Flex asked Toad. Then he turned to David. "Come on, man. You don't want to mess around with toads—you might get warts." He laughed and headed toward the door. David and the others followed.

"You can't get warts from a toad!" BB yelled

after them. "Idiots," he added under his breath. It seemed like BB couldn't stand to hear anything wrong being said about bugs *or* toads.

Graham and I both looked at Toad, who seemed upset at Flex's comment.

"I take it you and Flex don't get along too well," I said.

Toad forced a fake smile and said, "Flex is just fine. Everyone here is part of the Camp Grizzly family." Then he called out for everyone to follow him back to our cabins.

"So are you still going to get the bear claw?" Graham asked me.

I thought for a minute. I wasn't so sure that there were bears in China with stickers on their claws. "I don't know. I'll think about it."

"Well, I'm going to buy one," Graham said. "It will make me look tough at the marshmallow roast with the girls. Who cares what David thinks?" He paid for the claw, and we started walking back to the cabin.

"You know, just wearing this claw makes me

feel stronger," Graham said. He clenched his fists and flexed his arm muscle. "Oh yeah, much stronger," he added in a strained voice.

The look on his face was pretty convincing. I felt his flexed arm. I wasn't sure if I was feeling a muscle or not. It was kind of squishy.

"So you really think that makes you stronger?"

Graham pulled his arm away from my grasp. "Of course I do. Watch this." Graham walked over to a big rock on the side of the trail. It was about the size of a beach ball. He squatted down, put both arms around it, and tried to lift. After a few groans and other weird noises, he let go.

"This one must be cemented into the ground," he said. Then he searched for another smaller rock. This time he found one about the size of a bowling ball. Again, he bent over and gave it a heave, but it didn't budge either. Finally, he picked up a small rock the size of a baseball. "Yeah, check it out," he said.

"Wow, very impressive," I joked. We made our way back to the cabin.

All three of the cabins in our bear patrol stood around a large campfire pit. There were three long benches made from logs around the pit. I hoped we would be able to make a fire there. We took a seat on the benches.

I looked around at our bear patrol. Tiny and BB sat next to me and Graham. On another bench was a skinny kid named Carl who was picking his nose and a boy named Jackson who just stared at Carl picking his nose. A kid named Shawn and another named Kenny were sitting on the ground in front of the bench and playing in the dirt. There were four other kids on the last bench. They had their shirts pulled up and were trying to decide whose belly button stuck out the most. It didn't seem like any of us belonged in the popular crowd. Becoming popular was going to be harder than I'd thought.

Toad stood up on one of the benches. "Okay, gang, the first order of business is coming up with a name for our patrol. You guys don't want to be called 'those guys from cabins four, five, and six.'

So what do you think?" He looked at us and waited. Since we didn't know everyone in our troop yet, we were all a little nervous about saying anything. Finally Graham spoke up.

"How about the Bear Claws?" he said, holding up the claw hanging around his neck.

That kid Jackson raised his hand. "How about the Dinosaurs?"

Another guy yelled out, "Sharks?"

"How about the Arachnids?" BB shouted, jumping up. Everyone stopped and stared at him. "Or maybe not," he added. He quickly sat back down.

Then this kid named Kyle yelled out, "Let's be the Toads!" We all looked at him like he was crazy. He was kind of like a boy version of Lizzy, the biggest teacher's pet in my school. Toad seemed to like it though.

"Let's have a vote," Toad said. We all raised our hands as he repeated the different names. "It looks like the top two names are the Toads and the Bear Claws. So raise your hand if you want Bear Claws." There were six hands in the air. "Okay, how about the Toads?" Again six hands went up. "Hmm, a tie. Well, let's see. How about we compromise and call ourselves the Toad Claws?" We all sat there and looked at each other.

"Is he serious?" I said to Graham. But before anyone could figure out if he was serious, we were officially called the Toad Claws.

"I didn't even know toads had claws," Tiny said.

"Well, technically they don't," BB explained. "Unless you consider—"

"Now we need to come up with a patrol cheer," Toad interrupted.

"How about, 'Toad Claws are the best, just like Toad!'" Kyle said.

"Talk about a teacher's pet," I whispered to Graham.

"More like a counselor's pet." Graham chuckled. "Who is that kid?"

"You mean Lizzy-Boy?" I said. We both burst out laughing.

Shawn, one of the kids who was playing in the

dirt, got up and said, "Let's hop around like toads and hold our fingers in the air like a claw, like this." Then he jumped around holding his finger high in the air and bending it like a claw.

"Perfect!" Toad smiled. "Now just add a yell."

"How about 'Hooray Toad Claws!'" a kid called out.

Then Graham hopped up like a toad and yelled out, "Har! Toad Claws!" like a pirate.

"I like it," Toad agreed.

I wondered what the deal was with Graham and this pirate stuff. I looked over at BB and Tiny to see if they thought this was crazy too. But Tiny was already hopping around like a massive toad. I would have expected that, since he always seemed so happy. But even BB, who seemed a little more serious, was holding up his claw and cheering, "Har! Toad Claws," like Graham. I thought it was the craziest patrol name and cheer I had ever heard, but I joined in anyway.

"Har! Toad Claws!"

5

Smashed Toes and Cannonballs

AFTER A FEW minutes of jumping around like toad pirates, we were tired. We all straightened our claw fingers and took our seats back on the log benches.

"Okay, Toad Claws," said Toad. "Let me tell you what we have on the schedule this afternoon and tonight. In thirty minutes, you all have to be down at the lake to take your swim tests."

Kenny asked what a swim test was. Toad explained that we would each jump into the water out by the dock. Then we would have to swim the length of the dock and back three times. The first time you had to use a specific swim stroke, the forward crawl. The other two times you could use any stroke you liked.

"After the swim test you can get cleaned up for dinner. And each night after the day's activities the Toad Claws will meet back here for Roses, Thorns, and Buds."

"What's that?" I whispered to Graham.

"I don't know. We didn't do that when we were Cubs. Maybe it's some secret activity you can only do once you're a Grizzly."

All the Toad Claws ran into their cabins to get into their swimming trunks. I dug through my duffle bag but couldn't find my trunks.

"Hey, where are we supposed to change?" Graham said. "I'm not changing in front of you guys, that's for sure."

BB looked around the room. "Yeah, me neither. I'm going to the bathroom to change." The cabins didn't have a bathroom, so all of the campers shared a big bathroom next to the lodge. That's where the showers were too.

"Wait for me," I said. "I just need to find my suit."

Tiny had his entire bag dumped out in a pile on the floor. "Me too!"

Good idea, I thought. I dumped out my duffle bag as well and searched through the pile. Finally, Tiny and I both held up our trunks and exclaimed, "Found them!"

"It's about time," Graham said. "Let's go."

But instead of moving toward the door, Tiny stood and climbed to his top bunk. "I just need to grab my nose plug. I think I left it up here."

"Oh, man," Graham huffed. "We're never going to get out of here."

"Here it is. Let's go!" Tiny said. Then, before I could move, Tiny came flying off of the top bunk and landed right on my foot.

"Yeow!" I screamed. I fell to the floor and grabbed my foot.

Tiny bent down and held his hand out to help me up.

"Sorry, Raymond," he said. "Are you okay?"

I wanted to say, "Of course I'm not okay—you just landed on me," but I knew it wasn't his fault. He probably couldn't see my foot from up there.

"Yeah, I'm fine." I grabbed his hand and tried to stand up. The pain was awful. I hobbled around the room a bit, trying to "walk it off," as my baseball coach always said when someone got hit by a ball. Once some kid accidentally let go of the bat after he swung, and it hit our friend Carlos in the leg. He fell down and started to cry. I thought he should have gone to the doctor, but Coach just told him to "walk it off."

I tried to walk this off, but I could barely walk at all.

"Too bad you're not a baby spider," BB said, pushing his glasses higher onto his nose. "They grow new legs if one gets smashed or pulled off." I looked at BB and thought that I was really happy I wasn't a baby spider.

Tiny felt so bad that he even offered to give me a piggyback ride to the lake. It didn't seem like a bad idea. But after a minute or two, he got really out of breath, so Graham and I slowly walked the rest of the way while the others went ahead.

By the time we got down to the dock, my foot was feeling better. Tiny had just finished his swim test, and the lifeguard signaled for BB to jump in.

"Whoa, look at him go. BB's like a fish," I said. That kid could really swim. He finished his laps in no time at all.

Graham handed me his glasses. It was his turn. He jumped in and screamed, "It's freezing!" He swam much slower than BB, but finished just fine. After he got out, the lifeguard checked Graham's name off on a pad of paper and then pointed his pen at me.

"All right, you're up. Remember, the first lap is a forward crawl, and then you can swim the other two laps using any stroke."

Graham gave me a pat on the shoulder. "Good luck. It's a little chilly in there." I wasn't too nervous. I took swimming lessons when I was in first grade, and I was one of the best swimmers in my class.

"Cannonball!" I jumped in and splashed everyone. Graham was right, it was freezing. And each

time I kicked, my foot would hurt. I stopped for a moment to rest my foot after my first lap.

"Are you okay in there?" the lifeguard asked. "Do you need to stop?"

"No, I'm all right." I started again, but with every kick it hurt even more. I took one more quick break and then finished and pulled myself out. The lifeguard called me over. He told me that he couldn't check me off because I stopped twice.

"What? I didn't stop because I couldn't make it. I stopped because my foot hurt. I'll bet I could swim ten laps if my toes weren't smashed. I'm probably the best swimmer in my patrol!"

"I'm sorry," he said. "It's for your own safety. If your foot feels better you can try again tomorrow. Until then you can still play in the lake. You just have to stay in that area over there." He pointed to a small little roped-off place by the shore.

"Oh man. This stinks," I said.

Graham heard the whole thing. "At least you can still go into the water. Let's go check it out." We walked over to the roped-off area.

"Yeah, it's not so bad," I said. "Last one in is a rotten Toad Claw!" I ran over and jumped in. Unfortunately, instead of making a huge cannonball splash, I hit the bottom. Not only did my foot hurt now, but my bottom was bruised. I stood up, and the water was only a little higher than my knees. Graham had been running behind me, but after seeing me crash, he came to a screeching halt and waded through the water until he was at my side. The water reached a little higher on him, but not much.

"What's this all about?" he said. "You can't swim in here."

"I know. Why would they even have this shallow place?" We tried to think of something fun we could do there. We tried jumping up and down, but that wasn't fun at all. We tried sitting down, but that was like sitting in a big bathtub. Finally, we just got out and joined Toad and the rest of our group for the walk back to our cabin.

6

Extra Tighty Whities

"OKAY, TOAD CLAWS! It's almost everyone's favorite time of day: dinner!" Toad announced. "We have about thirty minutes if any of you want to shower off that lake water before you eat. Otherwise, you can have free time in your cabin."

I definitely wanted a shower. I felt like I had a bunch of dirt in my swimming trunks from my cannonball into the shallow water. Graham, Tiny, BB, and I all decided to shower. The rest of the guys thought they were clean enough already.

When we got to the showers a bunch of kids

were drying off and getting dressed. "Hey, these are the *boys'* showers," David said as we walked in. "No girls allowed." They all laughed.

"How come you're here then?" BB snapped back. He and Graham gave each other a high five. I shook my head, wondering why we always had to run into David.

"Just wait until the Olympics. Then you'll see who the real men are," David sneered.

"We'll see, all right," Graham said.

We set our clothes down on a bench and each took a shower stall. Tiny started singing one of the camp songs we had learned about a little green frog. Pretty soon we all joined in. After a couple more songs Tiny, BB, and I got out and dressed. Graham was still enjoying the hot shower after being in the cold lake.

"Come on, man," I told him.

"Just go ahead without me. I'll be there in a few minutes," he replied.

"Okay, we'll wait for you at the cabin." Graham just kept singing. BB and I started running back to the cabin. I thought Tiny was right behind us, but when I turned around, he was still near the showers walking really slowly.

"Hey, are you all right?" I called back to him. We stopped and waited for him to catch up.

"I don't know. I just feel a little uncomfortable," Tiny said. He had a sick look on his face.

"What do you mean?" I asked. He stood there for a moment trying to find the words to describe how he was feeling.

"It's probably nothing," he finally said. We walked back to the cabin. Tiny tried to sit down on BB's bunk, but it looked like he was having a hard time.

"What's wrong with you, Tiny?" BB asked.

"You didn't do a cannonball in the shallow part of the lake too, did you?" I said.

"No, it's just that—"

Just then Graham came busting through the cabin door. "Do I look smaller than I did this morning?" he interrupted.

"What are you talking about?" BB asked.

"Well, either my mom bought me some huge . . . um . . . clothes by mistake, or I have suddenly gotten puny."

I looked at Graham. "You don't look any punier than normal."

"That's so weird," Tiny said. "I feel the total opposite—like I got even bigger."

"You guys look the same to me," BB said.

"It just feels like my"—Tiny got quiet and whispered—"like my underwear is suddenly really small."

We stood there for a few moments trying to figure it out. Then BB snapped his fingers and adjusted his big glasses. He looked like a scientist who had just made a new discovery.

"You guys haven't gotten bigger or smaller. You're probably just wearing each other's—"

Then it hit us all at the same time. "Underwear!" we all shouted. "Ooh, gross!"

"No way!" Graham said. "I'm sure I didn't put on your underwear."

"Me neither!" Tiny cried.

Then Graham had an idea. "My mom wrote my name on mine. Check your tag."

Tiny could barely move. "They're so tight I don't think I can stretch them to see. But check yours. My mom did the same thing."

Graham pulled the back of the underwear around to the front without even stretching it. "It says TINY," Graham read in a horrified voice. "Oh gross, I'm wearing your underwear!"

Tiny grabbed a new pair of underpants from his bag and ran toward the door. "I'll meet you guys at the mess hall," he called out. He couldn't run very well in Graham's tight underwear. He looked like an enormous penguin trying to jog.

"Me too," Graham yelled, following Tiny. The back of his underwear where he had pulled it around was hanging out of his pants.

BB and I stood there laughing our heads off. Then at the same time we both looked at each other and stopped laughing. We must have had the same thought, because we both reached for the back of our underwear and twisted our necks around. We let out sighs of relief as we read our own names.

Graham and Tiny made it to the dining hall just as dinner started. They looked happier and much more comfortable. Dinner was spaghetti, applesauce, and salad. On the way to our table we passed by David and his patrol.

"Hey, it's the Geek Patrol," David called out. The rest of his table laughed. David had always been mean to me and Graham, but I didn't think his whole table would join in. I looked at Tiny, BB, and Graham. I wondered if we did seem a little geeky. I mean, even though Tiny was a big guy, he didn't look scary. Some kids look huge and tough. Tiny just looked huge and happy. You could tell just from looking at him that he would never hurt a fly. Then there was BB and his bugs, and Graham with his messy, curly red hair and his crooked glasses. I looked down at my clothes, which were hand-me-downs from my cousin Norman. I hated to admit it, but maybe we did look like geeks.

"How are those underpants fitting?" David yelled out. His entire table busted up.

"That was you?" Graham exploded.

"What's the matter?" David smirked. "Can't you read your own name on the tag?" I wanted to go tell Toad, who was in the front of the room talking to Fuzzy. But there was one thing I knew for sure: tattlers were *never* popular or cool. If we were going to be popular, we would have to try something else. Finally, we made our way to our table. Fortunately, it was far away from David's.

"This is going to be tougher than I thought," Graham said. "How can we convince everyone we're really cool when David's announcing that we're geeks?"

"I was just thinking the same thing. I can't believe that he switched your underwear. He must have done it when we were showering," I said. "What I wouldn't give to really get that guy."

"Yeah, me too," Graham agreed.

"Me three," Tiny said. Graham and I both looked at him. It seemed like such an un-Tiny thing to say. Tiny was usually so happy.

"Hey, nobody messes with my underpants," Tiny said.

"You know what? You're right," Graham announced. "Two can play that game. If he wants to pull pranks on us, he had better be prepared to get some pranks pulled on him too."

"Count me in," BB added. He adjusted his glasses. "I always stand by my bugs and my friends."

"We need to think of something good," Graham said, rubbing his hands together.

As we sat there planning our attack, there was a commotion at the table next to ours. A kid was standing on his seat to make an announcement.

"And now the moment you've all been waiting for! The Amazing Mark Herron will eat whatever we mix on his tray. Gather around, Grizzlies."

We got up and squeezed into the crowd that had already formed. A kid who must have been the Amazing Mark Herron was sitting at the table with a tray in front of him. He wore a Hawaiian shirt and a necklace made of what looked like little seashells.

"All right, dudes," Mark announced, "bring on the spaghetti." The first kid dumped a pile of spaghetti onto the tray. "Right on, dude," Mark said. "Now the applesauce." His friend scooped some applesauce on top of the spaghetti and stirred it in. A low "ooooh" came from the crowd. "Dude, bring on the salad." Salad was then mixed into the pile. Finally, the disgusting mixture was complete.

"What's with all the 'dude' talk?" I whispered to Graham.

"What do you mean? Cool guys like that guy always say dude," Graham answered. "Everyone knows that."

Mark lifted a spoonful of the nauseating concoction into the air and took a whiff. "It's Herron's Heap!" he said. "Any of you dudes care for a sample?" There were no takers. Then, without plugging his nose or making a face at all, he put the spoon in his mouth. He let out a big "Mmm" as he pulled the clean spoon from his lips. Everyone cheered. Mark stood up and took a bow. "We'll see you dudes next time for another exciting episode of Herron's Heap."

Even after the crowd broke up and everyone returned to their tables, the whole room was still talking about the Amazing Mark Herron.

"I can't believe he ate that!" I said. "He didn't even flinch. That was disgusting."

Graham agreed. "Yeah, that guy is so cool."

After dinner all the patrols gathered in front of the lodge. Fuzzy led us through a few songs, and the staff performed some more funny skits. Then, one at a time, each patrol presented its new name and cheer. Fuzzy said the patrol that showed the most spirit would get an award at the ceremony on Friday night.

We listened as each patrol performed. They all had cool names like the Fighting Eagles, Super Snakes, Roaring Lions, and stuff like that. Graham looked at me. "For some reason our name and cheer don't seem as cool now as they did earlier today."

"Yeah, I'm not sure they're going to help much with our popularity," I said.

Finally, it was our turn. Toad hopped up in

front of us. I was already embarrassed. "One, two, three," he called out. Then we all screamed, "We are the Toad Claws!" and hopped around cheering, "Har! Toad Claws!" The other patrols were either laughing or looking at us like we were nuts. No one laughed harder than Flex's team.

"Just what I would expect from a Toad," Flex called over to us. I could hear in his voice that he didn't mean it in a good way. Toad seemed to hear the comment but ignored him.

Flex's patrol was called the Muscular Monsters, and for their cheer they did four push-ups while yelling "One, two, three, four. Muscles are the best for sure!" Then they jumped up and flexed their muscles. I thought they looked stupid, but a lot of people cheered for them and thought they were cool. For some strange reason the crowd thought muscular monsters were cooler than pirate toads.

7

Campfire Chat

AFTER EVERYONE FINISHED their cheers, we sang a final song and lowered the flag. Our patrol followed Toad back to the benches in front of our cabins.

We all sat down, and Toad made a campfire in the pit. "All right, who's ready for Roses, Thorns, and Buds?"

We looked around at each other. I don't think anyone knew what he was talking about.

"Let me explain, Toad Claws. Every night when we gather around the campfire, we'll each take a turn and share a rose, a thorn, and a bud. A rose is something you've enjoyed that day, maybe your favorite activity or just something great that happened. A thorn is something that didn't go so well or that you didn't like about the day. And, finally, a bud is something that you are looking forward to tomorrow."

Toad looked around at our blank faces. "Why don't I go first to show you how it works? Today my rose was coming up with our patrol name and cheer with you guys. Patrols always choose to be eagles, hawks, or mountain lions, but this is the first time I've ever heard of one called the Toad Claws.

"As for my thorn . . . I'd have to say that my thorn was stepping in the mud this afternoon. These are my brand-new camp boots.

"And my bud is the hike we'll be taking tomorrow. It's always my favorite activity." Toad sat down at the end of the bench in front of cabin six and patted a kid named Jackson on the back. "Your turn," he said.

"Okay, my rose was watching Mark Herron eat the Herron's Heap at dinner. It was awesome!" A lot of heads nodded in agreement. "My thorn was the freezing cold water in the lake." Again, there were a lot of heads nodding. "And my bud is getting to see Herron's Heap again tomorrow."

Graham turned to me. "Raymond, these guys never met Mark Herron until tonight, and they already think he's the greatest."

"I know. I don't get it. All he did was eat a pile of mixed-up food," I said.

Graham was right. Almost every kid mentioned Mark Herron as a rose or a bud. One kid even had him as his thorn because he missed seeing Herron's Heap at dinner.

Finally someone got up who didn't adore Mark Herron: Lizzy-Boy.

"My roses, thorns, and buds are the same as Toad's," he said.

"You mean your thorn is that Toad stepped in the mud?" Graham called out. Everyone laughed, except Lizzy-Boy. He just gave Graham a rude smirk and then sat down.

I leaned over to Graham. "Wow, he really is like Lizzy."

At last it was our cabin's turn. Tiny went first.

"Well, my rose is making friends with the guys

in my cabin. They're really awesome." He looked down at us and smiled. It made me feel good. Then he continued. "My thorn is when I jumped off my bunk and accidentally landed on Raymond's foot. Sorry, man," he said to me. I smiled and gave him a thumbs-up. "And my bud would have to be the food. I really like to eat, if you can't tell." He pointed to his large stomach and everyone laughed.

BB was next. "Well, my rose is finding this cool brown spider I named Harry. I'm not sure what kind he is yet. He looks like a wolf spider, but he may be too small. But don't worry, I'll figure it out." I looked around, wondering how many people were actually worrying. "My thorn is when I forgot to tell Tiny about Harry and he got on Tiny's shirt. Sorry, Tiny." Tiny shivered, but smiled. Then BB raised both hands in the air. "And my bud is us winning the spirit award this week. Go Toad Claws! Har!"

The whole group joined in. "Har! Toad Claws!"

Graham stood up. "Let's see. My rose would have to be this awesome bear claw I got at the Trading Post." He held it up to show everyone.

"My thorn was when Tiny and I accidentally switched—"

Tiny jumped up and interrupted, "Wallets, when we accidentally switched wallets. Right, Graham?"

Graham caught the hint. "Um, yeah . . . wallets. It was really . . . um . . . weird." Everyone was looking at Graham like he was crazy. "My bud is having marshmallows with the girls tomorrow night. My girlfriend, Kelly, is coming from the girls' camp. Just in case you wanted to know."

It was my turn. "I guess my rose is just being here at camp. My thorn would be either that I didn't pass my swim test or that I did a cannonball in the shallow part of the lake." I rubbed my backside, which still hurt. There were a couple of chuckles from the patrol. "My bud is having this campfire every night. I love campfires."

In the end, I thought Roses, Thorns, and Buds was pretty fun. Afterward, we all sat around the fire for a while and chatted as, little by little, people went inside their cabins to go to bed.

Pretty soon it was down to BB, Tiny, Graham, and me. Graham and I ended up telling them about how we wanted to become cool and popular at camp.

"Are you guys part of the popular crowd at your schools?" I asked BB and Tiny.

"I'm actually the most popular kid at my school," BB said confidently.

"Me too," Tiny said. Graham and I stared at them in disbelief.

Then they both burst out laughing. "Just kidding! Of course I'm not," BB said.

"I hardly even know who the popular kids are at my school!" Tiny giggled.

I couldn't believe it. They sounded like they didn't even care that they weren't popular.

"Well, we're tired of being just regular guys," I said. "We want to be the guys that everyone likes and wants to invite to their parties."

"Yeah, like Mark Herron," Graham said.

BB shook his head. "Just because he calls everyone dude and eats some gross stuff, he's suddenly an instant hit? I'll bet he doesn't even know the life expectancy of a flea."

Then Graham stood up and hit himself in the forehead like he just remembered something. "Wait a minute. What if Mark *didn't* eat all of those weird things? And what if he didn't call everyone dude? What would he be like?"

I thought about that for a moment. "I don't know. Just some regular guy, I guess."

Graham smiled. "That's right, just a regular guy. A regular guy like us."

"Yeah, so what? You're not saying we should eat a bunch of weird things so people will think we're cool, are you?"

"Why not? It seems easy enough," Graham continued. "We could just throw a couple of things together on our trays and do what Mark did. And we could call everyone dude."

I thought about it. "I don't know," I said. "What if we just try calling everyone dude for a day? Maybe that would be enough and we wouldn't have to eat anything gross."

Graham rubbed his chin. "It's definitely worth a try . . . dude."

"All right, let's start right now, dude," I said. I

felt cooler already, like I wasn't just a regular guy anymore. I felt like, well, a dude.

I stood up. "Dude, I'm going to bed."

Graham yawned. "Yeah, let's go."

"Don't you mean, let's go, *dude*?" I said.

"Right. Thanks, dude."

BB and Tiny looked at us strangely. "Are you guys serious?" BB asked.

"Of course we're serious, dude," Graham replied.

Tiny stood up. "I think I'll pass on the whole dude thing," he said.

We all grabbed our toothbrushes and walked down to the bathrooms together.

"We've got to think of a great prank to pull on David," Graham said as we arrived at the sinks. We thought hard about what we could do, but none of us was really used to pulling pranks on people.

Tiny, BB, and I finished up in the bathroom and were waiting outside for Graham to come out when we heard him shout, "I've got it!"

"You've got what?" I asked.

Graham came out and announced, "This little trip to the bathroom has inspired me."

"What are you talking about?" I said.

Graham smiled and put one hand on my shoulder and the other on BB's.

BB slid his shoulder out from under Graham's hand. "Hey, did you wash those hands?" he asked.

"I've got one word for you guys," Graham said. We all leaned in to hear this one important word.

"*Toilet paper,*" he whispered.

"Toilet paper? But that's two words," Tiny said.

"No, it isn't," Graham argued. "*Toilet* is a word, and *paper* is a word, but when you are talking about toilet paper, it's just one thing. You know, *toiletpaper.*" He repeated the words really fast, trying to make it sound like only one word.

"Tiny's right," BB interrupted. "It is two words."

"That's okay," Tiny said. "It can be one word for Graham." Tiny never wanted to hurt anyone's feelings.

"Whatever. It doesn't really matter how many

words it is," Graham said. "The point is: we should toilet paper David's cabin."

I looked around to see if anyone else might have heard. "Are you crazy?" I whispered. I couldn't believe he was actually suggesting it.

"Count me in," Tiny said.

"What? You too, Tiny?" I dropped my head into my hands.

BB jumped up and down. "Me too! Let's do it."

All three of them were bouncing around now. I grabbed Graham by the shoulders and tried to stop his bouncing. "Wait a minute, you guys. What if we get caught?" I was getting nervous just thinking about this.

Graham just smiled. "Come on, Raymond. This is our chance to get David back. Haven't you always wanted to really get him?"

They all quietly chanted, "TP, TP, TP . . ."

"All right, all right, I'm in too," I finally agreed. They all slapped me on the back, and we headed back into the bathroom to find our ammunition.

8

Flying Toilet Paper

THERE WERE FOUR toilets in the bathroom, but we only took two rolls. We figured we had better leave a roll or two there. Graham and Tiny both hid a roll under their shirts, and we hurried back to our cabin. We stayed up and played cards, waiting for everyone else to go to bed. Toad came by and checked on us at around nine thirty.

"Lights out in five minutes," he said. We turned them off and climbed into our bunks, pretending to sleep. I did such a good job pretending that I actually fell asleep. Luckily, Graham woke me up.

"What time is it?" I mumbled. I couldn't tell if I had been asleep for five minutes or five hours.

"It's almost midnight," Graham said. "It's time to move."

I rubbed my eyes and got up. Slowly Tiny opened the door and we crept outside. There was just a sliver of a moon, and while the stars were bright, it was still really dark. We giggled softly, thinking about what we were about to do, and headed down the path. Suddenly, we heard a familiar voice.

"Hey, Toad Claws, what's going on?" It was Toad.

"Um, hi, Toad. Where are you going?" Tiny asked. Toad said he was on his way to the staff cabins. Then he asked us again what we were doing. I had a sick feeling inside. I knew we were busted.

"Okay," I said. "We were on our way to toilet paper the Muscular Monsters' cabins. Well, David's cabin." I was so nervous I started talking faster and faster. "It's just that David is so mean, and then today when he switched Tiny's and Graham's underwear, we just thought we'd—"

"Shhh." Toad put his finger to his lips. "You're going to TP the Muscular Monsters' cabins?"

"Yes, but we're sorry. We won't do it. Please

don't punish us," BB pleaded. We didn't want to get stuck cleaning the toilets, which is what happens if you get caught outside after lights-out.

"That's Flex's patrol," Toad said. He looked around and rubbed his hand through his hair.

"Well, just promise me you'll go straight back to your cabin after you're done."

We stood there, confused. It sounded like he was actually telling us to go ahead with our prank. Graham raised his hand like we were in school.

"Excuse me, but are you saying it's okay if we—"

"All I'm saying," Toad interrupted, "is that I never saw you tonight."

Toad began to whistle, and he started down the path to the staff cabins without saying another word. I remembered how Flex had made that mean comment about Toad earlier, and I wondered if Toad was secretly happy we were pulling a prank on Flex's patrol.

A few minutes later we reached David's cabin armed with our toilet paper. Graham wanted to be the first one to throw a roll. He was standing behind me. He pulled his arm way back, and Tiny, BB, and I looked up to see where the roll would go. Suddenly, I felt a smack on the back of my head.

"Ouch!" I yelled, in my loudest whisper. Graham had hit me with the roll of toilet paper. Luckily it was made of, well, toilet paper. Otherwise it would have really hurt.

"Sorry, *hermano*," Graham apologized. "I guess my aim was a little off."

I knew he was sorry because he called me *hermano*, which means "brother" in Spanish. We only use *hermano* when we're really serious, like when one of us is sorry for hitting the other one in the head with a roll of toilet paper.

Tiny picked up the roll. "Can I try?" he whispered. "I've never done this before."

"Sure," I said. "Try to throw it to the top of that tree." There was a tree right next to the cabin, and I thought it would help him to aim at it. Tiny looked awkward as he pulled his arm back. I could tell he probably didn't play baseball. But when he threw the toilet paper it flew through the air like it was shot from a cannon. It soared up and over the tree and just kept going until we lost it in the dark sky.

We all stood there and stared into the blackness. "Holy cow, where'd you learn to throw like that?" I whispered loudly.

Tiny held up his hands and examined them. "I don't know. I guess I don't know my own strength," he said. "I'll go find it." Tiny disappeared into the trees. BB had the other roll.

"So who wants to throw this one?" he whispered, holding it up.

"Go ahead," Graham said. "You do it." BB looked at the roll and then looked at the tree.

"Okay, ready or not, here goes." BB threw it perfectly, and it landed on one of the highest branches. But instead of unrolling as it fell, it just dropped down to the next branch and then fell onto the cabin roof. We all held our breath, hoping David and the others didn't hear the roll land.

"Oh great," I whispered. "That was our last roll."

BB hung his head. "Sorry, guys."

I tiptoed toward the woods where Tiny had

gone to find the other roll. I motioned for BB and Graham to follow. Tiny was still searching. We looked around for a few minutes but finally gave up.

"Hey, where's BB?" Graham said quietly. We looked around, but he was nowhere to be found. We walked back to the front of David's cabin and called BB's name softly. Suddenly we heard the door creak open. We were about to run when we saw BB tiptoeing out the door.

We froze in our footsteps. I couldn't believe BB was coming out of David's cabin. What had he been doing in there? We could see he was carrying something white in his hands. He had a big smile on his face. As he caught up with us, I realized he was carrying two pairs of underpants. We hurried away from the cabin and back to the main trail.

"No way." I laughed. "Are those what I think they are?"

"David's underpants. At least, I think they're his—they were under his bunk. Can you believe he only brought two pairs?"

"Nice work, BB." Graham high-fived him. "I didn't know you were so sneaky."

"Well, when you catch bugs you have to be very quiet and extremely quick," BB replied proudly.

"What should we do with them?" Tiny asked. We thought for a moment, then snuck over to the big statue of a bear standing upright by the lodge. We put one pair on his head like a winter hat and stuck the second on the front of the bear so it looked like he was wearing the underpants. We stood back and covered our mouths to muffle our laughter. Then we hurried back to our cabin.

We tried to fall asleep, but every time one of us drifted off, someone else would start giggling. Then we would recount the whole evening again. It was one of the best nights of my life.

9

A Grizzly Hike

I FINALLY CLOSED my eyes for what seemed like only a few minutes before I heard the morning gong. Toad was outside singing some song about getting out of bed. I think he was making it up as he went along. Tiny came bounding down from his bunk, and BB was already putting on his shoes and socks.

I stood on my bed to wake Graham up. He was snoring like crazy.

"Wake up!" I shouted.

"I didn't do it!" he mumbled, with his eyes still closed. "That bear already had underwear on his head." Finally, he woke up. "What's going on? What time is it?"

"It's morning. Time to go see if anyone has noticed the new wardrobe on the grizzly statue."

Graham immediately jumped up. We all got dressed as quickly as we could and ran outside.

"Good morning, Toad Claws!" Toad called out.

"Good morning, Toad!" we answered back.

"Did everyone sleep well?" Toad looked straight at us and smiled. Once the whole patrol was standing outside, Toad announced the day's activities: eating breakfast and then hiking up Mount Grizzly. That evening, the girls' camp would be joining us for a marshmallow roast at the big fire pit halfway between the cabins and the lodge.

"So let's go get some breakfast, Toad Claws." Toad led the way, hopping down the trail. I don't know how he always had the energy to hop around all the time. We all followed, but we got tired of hopping about halfway there and walked the rest of the way.

As we got closer to the lodge we saw a bunch of kids gathering around the statue and laughing their heads off. We didn't see David anywhere.

Fuzzy made his way through the crowd and

pulled the underpants off the bear. He turned and held one hand up to quiet the group.

"Okay, the show's over." I couldn't tell if he was angry or not. It kind of looked like he was holding back laughter.

"Does anyone know who these belong to?" He looked at the tag, but there was no name. Everyone looked around, but no one answered. I noticed Zach and a couple of the other Muscular Monsters giving each other looks. Fuzzy gave us a lecture on respect for others and about Grizzly pride.

"Well," he added at the end, "if any of you finds out you're missing your underwear, you can pick them up from the lost and found."

Aside from the brief lecture, I was relieved he didn't seem too mad. Toad walked up to us and said quietly, "You guys wouldn't know anything about this, would you?"

Graham and I looked at each other. "Well, let's just say the toilet paper didn't work out so well," Graham said.

"We're not in trouble, are we?" I asked.

Toad held up his claw finger, squinted one eye

like a pirate, and said, "Har, your secret's safe with me, Toad Claws." We both let out sighs of relief.

We got in line for breakfast with Tiny and BB. While we were eating Fuzzy announced that we all needed to be on our best behavior that night when the girls from Camp Wildflower visited. He said we had to let them get their marshmallows first, and also that we should offer to get them some punch. "Remember, they're our guests," he said.

Once we finished our breakfast, Toad gathered the Toad Claws together by the flagpole. He had two water bottles for each of us to bring on our hike. It was going to be a mile and a half up and a mile and a half back down. Then he gave us some great news.

"We will be hiking today with the Fighting Eagles."

I looked at Graham. "Do you know who's in the Fighting Eagles? Mark Herron!"

"This is perfect!" Graham said. "All we need to do is become friends with him, and popularity and coolness will be ours. Remember to say *dude* a lot." After all the TP and underwear excitement, I had forgotten about saying *dude*.

Just then Mark and his patrol showed up. Graham and I immediately headed over to him.

"Dude," Graham said. "Your show at dinner last night was amazing."

"Thanks, dude," Mark said, giving Graham a friendly fist bump.

"Yeah, I thought so too," I added. Graham gave me a stare like I was forgetting something. "I mean, I thought so too, dude," I said. Graham smiled and nodded.

We started up the trail. Along the way we stopped to look at certain plants that Toad pointed out and took a lot of breaks. We were only allowed to go as fast as the slowest hiker. That was usually Carl. About halfway up Mark took his shirt off and wrapped it around his head like a hat. Graham and I hurried to do the same. If that's what cool people like Mark did, then that's what we did.

Toad led us in some songs as we hiked. Toward the top it got really steep, and we were getting tired. Our singing slowed down until we were too tired to sing at all. Graham and I were even too tired to call each other *dude*.

But at last we made it to the top, and it was well worth the climb. It seemed like you could see forever. Toad and Twig, the Fighting Eagles' counselor, had brought sandwiches for all of us in their backpacks. We each found a rock or a log to sit on and ate. Graham and I sat on each side of Mark.

Just then a hawk flew over us and out into the open sky.

"Whoa, dude," Mark said, as we watched it soar farther and farther away.

"Duuude," Graham and I said together. The word *dude* began to take on a whole new meaning for us. You could use it any time. If you were amazed by something, instead of saying, "Wow, look at that. It's so cool," you could simply point and say, "Dude." And if you didn't like the sandwich you ate, which I didn't, you didn't have to say, "Yuck, that tasted terrible." You could just make

a sour face, shake your head, and say, "Duuuude" really slow, which I did.

As we started to head down the mountain, Mark turned to Graham. "Dude, you might wanna put your shirt back on. You're looking kinda fried." Graham was getting pretty red except for his freckles. They were turning green.

"Nah, I'm cool," Graham answered. I knew there was no way he was putting his shirt back on unless Mark did too.

When we made it back to camp, it was almost dinnertime. We had spent most of the day on the mountain. In the cabin, Graham finally tried to put his shirt back on, but by then he was so sunburned he could barely move.

"Check it out!" Tiny pointed to Graham's chest. There was a weird, pale shape in the middle of his sunburn. We all stared at it, trying to figure out where it had come from.

BB squinted at Graham's chest.

"It's from the bear claw necklace," he said, in his scientific-sounding voice.

"Wow," Graham said, looking at himself in the mirror. "I must be part bear now."

When we arrived at the mess hall, David immediately ran up to us.

"You guys are so dead," he said. "I know it was you!"

Graham shrugged. "What are you talking about?"

"My underpants on the statue!" David was fuming.

Toad ran up. "Hold on, everyone. Let's just calm down and eat dinner."

Now Flex appeared on the scene. "David, get back in line. I'll take care of this." He walked up to Toad. "I understand your little tadpoles were responsible for last night's prank. I expect an apology to the Muscular Monsters."

"What makes you think it was my guys?" Toad asked, although he knew it was us. "Did your boys do something to the Toad Claws that would make them want to play a prank on your patrol?"

Flex stood there, puzzled. He obviously didn't

want to admit that one of his boys pulled the first prank. "Well, I hope you guys had your fun. Because at the Olympics on Friday, you're going to wish you hadn't messed with us," Flex said.

"I don't know," Toad said. "I think you're going down."

Flex and his patrol laughed. "Lose to you guys? In your dreams."

"Oh yeah? I'll bet you the Toad Claws beat the Muscular Monsters," Toad offered confidently.

"You're on," Flex agreed. "What's the bet?" Just then David jumped forward.

"The bet is that the losers have to wear underpants on their heads to the award ceremony tomorrow night!" I looked around at the Muscular Monsters. Most of them were bigger than us, and probably stronger too.

I was just about to step up, apologize for what we did to David's underwear, and end this whole silly bet when BB shouted, "It's a bet!" The rest of the Toad Claws cheered.

"I hope we look good with underpants on our heads," I whispered to Graham.

10

Marshmallows with the Ladies

BEFORE DINNER WAS over everyone started gathering around Mark Herron's table as usual. But Mark stood up and announced, "Sorry, dudes. To welcome the girls to Camp Grizzly I will be performing at the marshmallow roast instead. See you there." Everyone was a little disappointed, but we all looked forward to seeing what he was going to eat at the campfire.

We all hurried outside to the big fire pit. Fuzzy was already there getting the fire started. He asked our patrol and the Super Snakes to bring some firewood over from the side of the lodge. One of the other patrols was setting up a table where the marshmallows and graham crackers would be, while another was putting out cups and filling them with punch.

Just as the fire got big, the girls came marching down the trail.

Graham jumped for joy and pointed. "There they are! Come on, Raymond! I mean, dude!" We hurried down to meet them.

We looked all over for the girls we knew, but couldn't see anyone. Then we heard a familiar voice behind us.

"Wow, look at those scary Grizzlies." It was Heidi, standing there with Diane.

Diane rubbed her hand through Graham's hair. "Yeah, but this one looks kind of puny. And I've never seen a Grizzly with red hair and a bad sunburn."

"Dude, careful with the hair," Graham said.

"Dude?" Diane laughed.

"Yeah, dude," Graham repeated. "That's what we call people. Dude."

"Okay . . . dudes." Heidi smirked, then she and Diane giggled.

"What's wrong with saying dude?" I asked. "A lot of people say dude and think it sounds cool."

"Sure, whatever . . . dudes," Diane said. They giggled again. Graham and I looked at each other. I could tell he was thinking what I was thinking: that Heidi and Diane were making fun of us.

"And you're wearing a necklace now?" Diane added, pointing to Graham's bear claw.

"Of course," Graham answered. "A lot of dudes, I mean guys, wear them." Diane bent over to get a closer look.

"Where's Kelly?" Graham asked.

"What are you talking about?" Diane asked. "Kelly went to Camp Hidden Meadows. Didn't I tell you that?"

"No, you just said that you, Heidi, and Kelly were all going to camp." He looked heartbroken.

"Oops, sorry," Diane said. She didn't sound very sorry though.

"Last one to roast a marshmallow is a rotten dude!" Heidi called out, before running to the fire. Diane was right behind her. Graham and I just stood there.

"Okay, now I know they're making fun of us," I told Graham.

"Well, maybe dude is something that just boys think is cool. Maybe it doesn't work with girls."

After spending our marshmallows on sticks, we grabbed a couple of extras and ran over to Diane and Heidi. I started roasting my marshmallow.

"You're holding it too close to the flame," Diane said. "It's going to catch on fire."

"Will not," I said. Just then my marshmallow went up in flames.

Diane hit me on the shoulder. "See, I told you."

I kept it in the fire. "Well, I like it that way, all crisp and—" Unfortunately, before I could finish my sentence, my marshmallow fell off the stick and into the fire.

Heidi burst out laughing. "That's probably the way you like it too, all dirty and melted onto a burning log."

I finally gave in. "Okay, maybe it's just a tiny bit too burnt."

"Yeah, kind of like Graham here," Diane said, slapping Graham on the back.

"Yeow!" Graham yelled.

While we all roasted another marshmallow, Tiny and BB walked up.

"Hello," Tiny said. "I'm Tiny."

"If you're tiny, then what's he?" Diane said, pointing to Graham. We all laughed, except for Graham.

"No, his name is Tiny," Graham said.

BB adjusted his glasses and cleared his throat. "And I'm BB. I like bugs."

"Nice to meet you, BB. I'm Heidi, and I don't like bugs," she said with a smile.

"Then you must be Graham's girlfriend," BB said to Diane.

"I don't think so!" Diane snapped.

Heidi laughed. "Graham doesn't have a girlfriend!" she told BB.

"What do you mean?" BB turned to Graham, whose sunburn had suddenly gotten even redder. But before he could say anything, a shout came from the other side of the campfire.

"The moment has arrived!" Mark Herron's friend announced, standing on a rock. "The Amazing Mark is about to eat tonight's Herron's Heap."

"Who's the Amazing Mark?" Heidi asked.

"Just some kid who eats anything," I said. "It's kind of sick."

"I want to see." Heidi pushed her way to the front of the crowd. Diane stayed back since she was tall enough to see over everyone.

"All right, dudes," Mark said. "I will begin with an ordinary graham cracker." He held up the cracker above his head. Then he took a napkin out of his pocket and opened it up. It looked like he had squished a bunch of food from dinner in there.

"Now we will add the heap." He set some peas on the cracker and smashed them so they wouldn't fall off. Then he put on a piece of chicken and smothered it in applesauce. "Dude, marshmallow, please." His friend brought over a freshly roasted marshmallow, which Mark placed on top of the mess. Then just before eating it he shouted, "And what goes better with graham crackers than milk?" He poured some milk over the hideous cracker sandwich and took a huge bite.

There were a lot of oohs and aahs from the crowd. I thought the girls would be grossed out, but they weren't. When the boys started chanting Mark's name, the girls joined right in. Mark took one more bite out of the cracker creation. It was dripping down his chin. Everyone cheered.

Pretty soon it was time for the girls to go. Diane and Heidi couldn't stop talking about the Amazing Mark.

"Didn't you hear how many times he said *dude*?" I asked. "I thought you guys hated that." Heidi and Diane looked at each other.

"I didn't notice," Heidi replied.

Diane shook her head. "Me neither."

When we got back to the cabin, everyone was ready for Roses, Thorns, and Buds. It seemed like all of the roses were either the hike up to Grizzly Peak or the Amazing Mark and his disgusting s'more.

Carl was the last kid to share. He pulled his finger out of his nose and stood up. He cleared his throat and said, "My rose was everything we did today. And my thorn is the word *dude*. No offense to some of you who are calling everyone *dude*, but I just can't take it anymore. It's driving me nuts." A couple of other guys nodded their heads, but no one looked directly at us. Then Carl took a deep breath and continued, "And my bud is everything else we're doing tomorrow."

Toad went last. He stood up and said, "My rose is the great hike we went on today. You guys are such an awesome patrol. I guess my thorn is getting you involved in that silly bet with the Muscular Monsters."

"It's okay, dude. I mean, Toad," Graham said. Then he mouthed "Sorry" to Carl.

"No, I should have been a better example to you guys. But that brings me to my bud: seeing Flex and the Muscular Monsters wearing their underpants on their heads Friday night!"

We all jumped up and cheered. "Har! Toad Claws!" we yelled, hopping in circles. After last night's adventure and today's hike, we decided to call it an early night.

Just before Graham and I stood up, Toad came over and sat down by us.

"Hey, guys. I just want you to know I've really enjoyed having you in my patrol. I don't know where all this dude stuff came from, but let me give you some advice." Graham and I leaned in toward him.

"Just be yourselves, and don't try to be like anyone else. We've got a great patrol, and you've made a lot of friends here who like you for who you are. That's what camp is all about. Remember that." Then he got up and walked down toward the lodge.

I looked at Graham. "What's that supposed to mean? How can the Amazing Mark get away with calling everyone *dude*, and when we do it, all of a sudden people think we're not being ourselves?"

"I know," Graham said. "It's like everyone's saying that Mark can say *dude* because he's cool. But us, no way—we're geeks and should only say geeky things. I can't believe Carl complained about us. I wish I could say my thorn over again. I'd say it was seeing Carl pick his nose all the time."

"Oh well, I guess we should stop saying *dude*. Heidi and Diane thought it was weird too."

Graham lowered his eyebrows and looked me square in the eyes. "No way," he said. "No one's going to tell me what it means to be myself. Maybe being myself is saying *dude*. Or maybe I'll want to eat a mixture of gross stuff tomorrow at lunch. Actually, that's exactly what I'll do tomorrow."

"Not me. I think I'd puke." I shivered just imagining it. "I guess maybe I'm fine with not being cool."

"Come on, *hermano*," Graham said. "We don't have to spend our lives being geeks. If we want to be the Amazing Raymond and Graham, then what's stopping us? Wouldn't you like to hear the entire lodge chanting our names after dinner?" I thought about it for a minute. That would be pretty cool.

"It would be awesome to be the most popular kids at camp," I told Graham. "But I don't know if I'm willing to eat that junk to make it happen."

"Of course you are, man!" Graham got up and stood right in front of me. "We can do this. We're a team, like Mark and that other guy." Graham paused for a moment. "Wow, he's the second most popular kid in camp, and no one even knows his name. It's always Mark Herron and that other guy."

"Yeah, weird." I shook my head.

"Wait, that's it, Raymond," Graham said. "This is what we're going to do. I'm going to be the other guy, and I'll announce you after dinner. Then I'll mix up a bunch of stuff for you to eat."

"What? Why me? Why can't *you* eat that stuff and *I'll* be the announcer?" I wasn't sure how this conversation suddenly turned from Graham being willing to eat the gross mixture to him announcing and me eating it.

"It has to be you," Graham said. "It's just like in baseball. I was the catcher trash-talking behind the plate, getting the batter nervous, so you could come in for the kill with your awesome fastball." I wasn't sure that these two situations were the same, but somehow hearing about my fastball made me feel strong, like I could do anything.

"You're right! We have just as much right as Mark and that other guy to be popular. Tomorrow night those guys are in for some competition."

Graham and I swung our hands up in the air to give each other a high five, but we missed. "It's just getting dark," Graham said.

"One thing though," I said. "I know no one can tell us not to say *dude*, but I kind of agree with Carl."

"No problem. I hate to admit it, but I'm getting sick of it too," said Graham. We went into the cabin and said goodnight to BB and Tiny without using the word *dude* at all.

11

Raging Raymond

UNLIKE THE NIGHT before, we slept like logs. We were so tired we didn't even hear Toad's song in the morning. He had to come into our cabin and wake us up.

We were all excited about today. This was our day at the lake. After breakfast, David's patrol would be on their hike most of the day, so we wouldn't have to see them at all. I was hoping I'd get to retake my swim test. My foot felt completely better, and I knew I could pass it this time.

We got dressed and went to the mess hall for breakfast. It was cereal, muffins, and fruit today. The Muscular Monsters walked in behind us.

"Hey, Toad Claws. You'd better save a pair of

clean underpants for Friday. You're going to need them."

We just ignored David and sat down by the Fighting Eagles. Graham sat next to me and told me I should practice mixing my food up and eating it.

"Good idea," I said. I had a banana, so I cut some pieces up and put it in my cereal. Then I put in a couple of strawberries too. "Okay, here goes," I said. I put a big spoonful in my mouth, prepared for the disgusting taste. It was actually pretty good. "Hey, I'm going to be good at this. It's not bad."

"What do you mean? You just have cereal and fruit. That stuff always goes together." Graham shook his head. He grabbed the salt and pepper shakers and started sprinkling them in my bowl. Then he pulled off a piece of his muffin and dropped it in.

"Try that." He took my spoon and stirred it all up.

I looked at the soggy mess and decided to pass. "I'm kind of full," I said. "Plus, I don't think you're supposed to eat too much before you go swimming." I picked up my tray and brought it over to the cleaning area. Then I grabbed a new muffin for the road.

We spent almost the entire morning in the lake. Fortunately, I was able to take my swim test again, and I passed. There were huge tubes to play on and a big rope that you could swing on before dropping into the water.

Toad stayed and swam with us too. He had this crazy swimsuit that was like a tank top and swimming trunks all in one. No one could swing higher than Toad on the rope. He swung really high and yelled "Yahoo!" as he flew through the air.

"It's Superbug to the rescue!" BB screamed, as he swung out over the water. He even did one flip after he let go of the rope. Graham tried a flip too, but he landed on his sunburned back.

By the time lunch came, we were starving. They were serving chili and cornbread. Our patrol decided to eat outside on the grass under a big tree.

Graham had a grin on his face. "You guys know what chili does to you, don't you?" he said.

"Do I ever," Tiny said. "You guys are in for a

smelly time tonight." The look on Tiny's face made me a little scared to sleep in the cabin with him.

After lunch we spent the afternoon in arts and crafts making dream catchers, weaving string across these wooden hoops in whatever design we wanted. They're supposed to catch bad dreams.

"With this, I'm going to have sweet dreams of Kelly every night," Graham announced.

"And I'm going to dream of catching every bug on the planet," BB said.

Tiny shivered. "Not me! That would be a nightmare. I hope my dream catcher stops all of those bug dreams from getting into my brain."

Carl said he wanted to have dreams about living in a huge chocolate house that he could just pick at and eat all day long. That made sense to me, since he seemed to like picking things.

As dinnertime rolled around I was getting nervous. In the food line, I said to Graham, "Do you really think I should eat all that gross stuff?"

"Trust me, Raymond. Sometimes you have to do things you don't like if you want to be cool."

"I'm just getting a little nervous."

"Just imagine all those kids chanting your name. 'Raymond, Raymond,'" he whispered in my ear. He was right. Eating a little bit of gross food would be worth having everyone like me.

We loaded our trays and sat down. I didn't eat very much for fear that I would throw up when I ate the mixture afterward.

"Now, how should I announce you? I can't call you Amazing Raymond. Mark already has *amazing* in his name. It needs to start with an *R*, like Raymond. How about Rainy Raymond?"

"Rainy Raymond?" I said. "That doesn't even make sense."

"Just brainstorming. What are some other *R* words? *Ripple, ring, run, robot, raging.* That's it: Raging Raymond."

"Raging Raymond," I repeated. "I like it."

Just then, Mark's friend announced, "The Amazing Mark is ready for his nightly show!"

"Dang," Graham said. "I wanted to go first. Oh well, these kids can't get enough of this stuff. We'll do it right after."

Dinner had been tacos and more applesauce.

Mark took his shell and loaded it with meat, mustard, applesauce, and salad dressing, and poured on some milk. I was gagging just watching Mark mix it up. The sick mixture was oozing out of the ends of the taco.

A loud "ooh" filled the lodge as he bit into it. It was his best performance yet. As people started leaving, Graham jumped up on the bench.

"Don't leave, everyone. Round two is about to begin, featuring Raging Raymond and his Spoonful of Doom!" Unfortunately, no one seemed to care. A few people looked over at Graham as they left, but they didn't stop.

"Don't you mean, 'featuring Raymond the Dork'?" David yelled over from across the room.

Graham rubbed his hand through his hair, then exclaimed, "Wait, people! Tomorrow night you will see something *really* amazing. Raging Raymond is not going to eat a simple mixture of food. Instead he will eat . . . A WORM!" Suddenly everyone stopped and turned back.

"That's right, Grizzlies—a worm straight from the Camp Grizzly dirt." Graham motioned for me to stand up. Instead, I pulled him down.

"See you all tomorrow!" Graham shouted from his seat.

"What are doing?" I cried. "Why did you promise everyone that I would eat a worm?" I put my head on the table and closed my eyes. There was no way I was ever going to eat a worm. As I sat there wondering how Graham could do this to me, his best friend, I heard the sound I had dreamed about.

"Raymond, Raymond!" they were all chanting. I looked up and everyone was gathering around our table.

I stood up and waved at everyone.

"Yes, tomorrow night I will eat a worm!"

Mark came up to me and gave me a high five. "Dude, this will be awesome! The Amazing Mark eating Herron's Heap and then Raging Raymond eating a worm for dessert. We are quite the team, dude."

"See," Graham said. "I knew it! We're the talk of camp. How does it feel?"

"Incredible," I said. "It feels incredible."

After dinner we all gathered in front of the lodge by the flagpole. Each patrol yelled its cheer, trying to show they had the most spirit. And of course, we sang a few more songs. Afterward, Toad had to go to a staff meeting, so we had to have Roses, Thorns, and Buds without him. Unfortunately, we weren't allowed to start a fire by ourselves. We all brought out our flashlights instead. As each Toad Claw stood up to speak, the rest of us pointed our flashlights at him, like a spotlight.

Almost everyone's bud was that they were looking forward to seeing me eat a worm the next night. It was so different from the last night, when everyone was mad about hearing us say *dude* all the time. Now everyone thought we were the greatest, and all it took was promising to eat a worm.

Wait a minute, I thought. As I sat there listening to everyone sing my praises, I suddenly realized that I was really going to have to *eat a worm*!

12

Let the Games Begin

THE NEXT DAY was going to be either the best day of my life or the worst. Not only did I have the worm thing, but we would have to pay up if we lost our bet with David's patrol. The rest of the Toad Claws were excited about the Olympics. They weren't nearly as nervous as I was about losing and having to wear underpants for hats.

That night I couldn't sleep. I wanted to talk to one of my cabinmates, but Graham and Tiny had fallen asleep the second their heads hit the pillow, and BB was lying awake in bed but said he didn't feel like talking. He seemed upset about something, but I didn't know what.

I must have finally fallen asleep, because all of a sudden the gong startled me awake. At breakfast, the whole dining hall was buzzing about the Olympics. Even the staff was excited. Fuzzy stood in front by the fireplace and asked, "Who thinks they're going to win the Olympics?"

Everyone screamed and cheered. Then Fuzzy explained how the Olympics would work. There would be six different events. Each team would choose two people to compete in each event. The events were running, swimming, a log toss, an archery shoot, a rope climb, and an obstacle course. He held up a big map of the camp that showed where each event would take place.

"This is going to be awesome," Graham said. "The only thing better than seeing David's underpants on the Grizzly statue will be seeing them on his head after he loses."

"Do you really think we can win?" I asked.

"Of course I do," Graham answered with confidence. "Just look at our team."

I looked over at BB, who was standing on his

tiptoes trying to see the map Fuzzy was holding. Tiny was turned backward, not even paying attention. Carl was picking his nose as usual, only this time he was using his pinky. And Lizzy-Boy had his arms pulled inside his T-shirt with only his hands sticking out of the armholes. He was pretending he had really short arms.

"I hope you're right," I said.

Fuzzy dismissed us and we all got together with our patrols to decide who would compete in each event.

"I think BB should definitely do the swimming," I suggested. "He's like a fish."

BB took a bow and said, "Thank you, thank you." Toad wrote his name down.

"What about the rest of you guys?" Toad asked. At first, no one said anything. Finally Carl volunteered for running. After that, everyone started shouting out what events they wanted. I chose the obstacle course with Graham. Tiny didn't choose anything, so he got stuck with the rope climb.

"Are you all right with the rope climb?" Toad

asked. I think he wondered if Tiny could pull his big body all the way up the rope.

"I'm fine with it," Tiny said cheerfully.

The competitor that came in first place in each event would get three points, the second-place competitor would get two, and the third-place competitor would get one. After all the games were played, the points would be totaled, and the team with the most points would win.

The footrace was the first event. Carl and Lizzy-Boy were our runners. The race was from the lodge to the lake and back again, so we all gathered near the starting line in front of the lodge.

My stomach was churning with nerves.

"Okay, guys," Toad said to us. "Remember, we're just in this for the fun of it. But also keep in mind that if we lose, we'll be wearing you-know-what on our heads to the closing ceremonies. But be sure to have fun." Toad looked really nervous about the bet.

Fuzzy stood at the starting line and held up a cap gun. He shouted, "On your marks, get set . . ."

Then he shot the gun, and the runners were off.

"All right, Carl has the lead!" Graham yelled. All the patrols cheered for their runners. From our spot, we could see the runners until they were halfway to the lake, where the trail curved out of view. We stood and waited. It seemed like they were gone forever. Then suddenly they came running back around the trees.

"Hey, where'd Carl go?" I said. He was nowhere to be seen. Neither was Lizzy-Boy, for that matter. Zach was on David's team and, as I should have expected, he was now in the lead. Zach is the fastest kid in my school.

As they crossed the finish line, Fuzzy announced the teams of the first-, second-, and third-place competitors. "Muscular Monsters, Fighting Eagles, and Roaring Lions."

I felt something on my head and quickly turned around. It was David with his hands on my head. "What are you doing?" I said, moving away.

"Just measuring. I hope your underpants can fit over that huge head of yours." He laughed that obnoxious laugh and walked away. Carl came in sixth place, and I guess Lizzy-Boy must have just stopped running, because he never came back. We didn't see him again until we got to the lake for the next event.

The swimming race course went from the dock to a big buoy and back. This time Twig had the starting gun. As soon as it went off, BB was in the water. I knew we would do well in this race, and I was right. BB won by a mile. The Super Snakes came in second and the Roaring Lions took third.

The last event before lunch was the javelin throw, where you throw a long stick as far as you can. The farthest throw wins.

One of our guys from cabin four came in third for one point. "I wish they had a toilet paper toss," I told Graham. "Tiny would win that for sure." Mark Herron's friend, that other guy, could really throw that stick. He threw it at least ten feet farther than anyone else. David's team came in second. So now they were ahead of us by one point.

Fuzzy announced that we would be taking a break until after lunch.

In the lodge, we watched him adding up the

points and writing them on a big whiteboard with markers. The Muscular Monsters were tied for first place with the Fighting Eagles, we were in second place, and the Super Snakes and Roaring Lions were tied for third.

"We've just got to win this," I said.

"We will," Tiny said, "'cause we're good guys, and like they say, good guys always finish first."

"I think the saying is that good guys always finish last," BB said.

"Really? Last?" Tiny mumbled to himself. "That doesn't really make sense."

"Well, we just need to end up ahead of the Muscular Monsters. There's no way I'm wearing underpants on my head," Graham said. "Let's go eat."

We had submarine sandwiches for lunch. I tried not to eat too much so I wouldn't get a stomachache in the obstacle course, but they were so good I couldn't help myself, and I ended up eating two.

The next event was the archery contest. We had Shawn and Kenny from cabin six competing for us. Each participant had three arrows to shoot at a target. Whoever got his arrow closest to the bull's-eye would win. Neither of our guys looked like he knew how to shoot an arrow, but we cheered both of them on anyway.

Kenny's first arrow went over the target and into the woods, his second went straight into the dirt, and his third hit the target of the kid next to him, so it didn't count.

"Wow, that stinks," I said. Shawn wasn't much better. He hit the target with his first arrow, but only on the corner. His second arrow hit the ground, and his third actually made it close to the bull's-eye but then fell out, so we didn't get any points. The good thing was that David's team only got one point for coming in third.

The next event was the rope climb. I figured Tiny would need a miracle to pull himself up the rope, which was tied to a giant tree branch. At the top there was a bell you had to ring. And below, a camp counselor stood to time everyone with a stopwatch. Whoever climbed the rope and rang the bell fastest would take first place for his team.

David's team went first. One of their guys made it up in fifteen seconds and the other in twelve. The Super Snakes' best time was eleven seconds. The rest of the teams all did over fifteen seconds. Finally it was our turn.

Jackson went first. He was tall and skinny and climbed really fast. Unfortunately his time was sixteen seconds.

Some of the kids laughed a little when Tiny stepped up to the rope. He grabbed a hold and looked up at the bell. "Are you ready?" the counselor asked.

"I guess so," Tiny answered.

"Go!" the counselor yelled. In no time at all, Tiny was halfway up the rope. His hands were moving one over the other like some sort of monkey's. In eight seconds he had rung the bell and was on his way down.

We went crazy, cheering for him. "Where'd you learn how to do that?" I asked.

He shrugged his shoulders.

"That was the first time I'd ever climbed a

rope," he said. Tiny won first place. With that win and the Monsters taking third, we were suddenly tied for first place with the Muscular Monsters.

It was time for the final event. We all gathered around the starting line of the obstacle course. Fuzzy explained that this event was a team race. The two players from each team would have their times added together.

Our team gathered around me and Graham for a huddle.

"Okay, guys, this is it," Toad said. "Don't worry about the time. Just go as fast as you can. And remember, no matter what happens, you'll always be Toad Claws."

Graham and I walked over to the starting line with the other racers.

"I thought he was going to say, 'no matter what happens, you'll always be winners,' not Toad Claws," I whispered to Graham.

David and a short kid were racing for the Muscular Monsters. Gopher had us pick numbers from a hat to decide who would go first. Graham chose, and our team was last. David's was first.

"Okay, *hermano*. We can do this," I said. "We're faster than all these guys."

"I don't think I'm faster than that guy," Graham said, pointing to a guy on the Roaring Lions who looked like he was fourteen years old.

"Whoa, you're probably right," I said. "But we only have to be faster than them." I pointed to the Monsters.

The short kid went first. He tripped once while running through the tires, but other than that he ran a fast race. David stepped up to the starting line.

"Don't trip!" Graham yelled.

"Hey, your shoes are untied," Tiny yelled. David looked down.

"Ha-ha! Made you look." Tiny laughed.

"Your zipper's down," BB called out.

"That's enough," Flex told BB.

"But his zipper really is down," BB said. We all looked. He was right.

When the gun sounded, David was off in an instant. He hopped easily through the tires. He had a little trouble crawling through a long tube, but he climbed over the rock wall fast and made it to the finish line one second faster than his partner. Their combined time was forty-nine seconds. We were the last team to go. The Monsters were in third place in this event and would get one point if we didn't beat them.

"Why don't you go first, Raymond," Graham said when it was our turn. "I'm too nervous." I was nervous too, but I agreed. I took my place at the starting line.

"Hey, your shoe's untied," David shouted.

"Very original," BB commented, just loud enough for David to hear.

I wasn't going to let anything distract me. When the gun sounded I ran like the wind. I swerved in and out of the tires and dove through the tube. And climbing the rock wall felt so natural. I slipped once running between some big orange cones on my way to the finish line, but I still made good time. I finished in twenty-one seconds. Graham just needed to finish in twenty-nine seconds for us to beat the Monsters in the Olympics.

Graham looked scared. He walked up to the starting line and got down into position.

"On your mark, get set—"

"Hold on a minute," Graham said, stopping the counselor with the stopwatch. Then he stepped back and bent over and stretched.

"Hey, he can't stop," David complained. The counselor ignored David and waited for Graham to get ready again. Finally, Graham walked back up to the starting line. He did a couple of quick jumping jacks and then cracked his knuckles. I wondered how that would help him go faster, but I figured it probably couldn't hurt.

"Okay, I'm ready," Graham said. He got back down into starting position and gave the counselor a thumbs-up.

"On your mark, get set . . ." The shot rang through the air and Graham was off. I'd never seen Graham move so fast. He made it through the tires and tube like they weren't even there. The

Muscular Monsters stopped talking and stared at Graham as he flew through the course.

"Go, Graham!" the Toad Claws cheered.

After the tube, Graham raced to the rock wall. He reached up and grabbed a high rock. Unfortunately, as he put his foot on a lower rock, he slipped and fell. But he jumped up and was back on the wall in an instant. About halfway up he tried to grab another rock that was just out of his reach, and he slid down again.

"Hurry, Graham, hurry!" we screamed. Now we were nervous, and David's team was cheering.

Graham had been so fast until then that I thought he had some time to spare. But after he finally made it over the wall and ran through the cones and across the finish line, the timekeeper called out, "Thirty-three seconds."

We had lost by four seconds.

Silence fell over the Toad Claws. We knew exactly what those four seconds meant. Tiny put his huge hands over his face. BB shook his head and kicked up some dirt. Even Toad let out a big sigh.

As I looked at my team, I could picture them all with underpants on their heads.

"Great run, Graham," Toad said to Graham, patting him on the back. "You were really close!" We all joined in and congratulated him.

"But we lost. And it's all because of me," Graham muttered, hanging his head.

"It's not your fault," Tiny said. He put his huge arm around Graham's shoulder. "We're a team. This was just one event. We win or lose as Toad Claws."

"See you back at the award ceremony," David called. "And don't forget to wear your new hats!" The Muscular Monsters hooted and hollered all the way back to the lodge.

13

Humiliating Hats

"I CAN'T BELIEVE this," Graham told me back at the cabin. "What a total disaster. Not only have we not become cool, but now we have to humiliate ourselves in front of the entire camp by wearing underpants on our heads. Maybe you were right, Raymond. Maybe we are just supposed to be geeks, dorks, nerds, or whatever other unpopular name you can think of."

I tried to think of something to cheer him up. Usually he was the one who believed that everything was going to work out.

"No way, *hermano.* Who was the guy who said we can be as cool as we want to be?" I asked. Graham just gave me a blank stare.

"It was you, Graham. We still have a chance to be cool. Don't forget about my worm eating tonight. You heard it yourself at Roses, Thorns, and Buds. We'll be even bigger than Mark."

Graham started to nod his head. Then a full-blown smile stretched across his face. "You're right! We are going to be the hit of the camp. Thanks, *hermano*!"

The truth was, I had really been hoping to pass on the worm eating, but seeing Graham so depressed made me think I'd better do it.

About half an hour before dinnertime, we were back at the cabin getting ready. Everyone was a little sad that camp was almost over. Tiny sat quietly on his bunk drawing pictures. BB seemed especially sad. He hadn't said much since the Olympics ended, and he wouldn't even look at us. I wasn't sure what his problem was, because he wouldn't tell us when we asked him.

"Okay, *hermano*," Graham said. "This is it. Let's go find your dessert." He had a paper cup in his hand to put the worm in.

Finally BB stood up and cried out, "So you're really going to eat a harmless living creature just to be popular?"

Suddenly, I realized what had been bothering him. BB loved all sorts of small creatures. Our announcement that I was going to eat a worm must have been killing him.

"How could you do it?" he continued. "What did an innocent little worm ever do to you? You probably don't even know how good they are for the soil." He was really upset. I felt like I had just ruined his entire week.

"I'm so sorry, BB," I said. I looked up at Tiny, who seemed really sad too. He jumped down and put his arm on BB's shoulder. Graham and I looked at each other, not sure what to do. The entire camp would be waiting for our show tonight. Couldn't BB understand that? This was our chance to be the most popular kids in camp. I couldn't let this moment slip by. I mean, it was just a worm.

"BB, I can't tell you how sorry I am. But I hope one day you'll understand how important this is to us." I didn't know what else I could say.

"Come on, Graham." We headed for the door with our heads hung low. Graham tried to pat BB on the shoulder, but he moved away.

Outside Graham and I began our search for the worm.

"I feel terrible," I told Graham, as we looked under a big rock. There were a lot of bugs there, but no worms. We tried some others.

"He'll get over it, won't he?" Graham said. "Hey, there's one!" Graham grabbed the worm before it could squirm away.

"He may not like us anymore, but he'll get over the worm." I sat down on the ground and looked at the worm wiggling around in the cup.

"Just think about it this way, Raymond. BB may hate us, but think of all of the other kids who will love us." I could hear in his voice that Graham wasn't so sure that this was a good idea after all. It sounded like he was trying to talk himself into it.

"Yeah, all the other kids will like us." I paused for a moment to gather my thoughts. "But we don't even know those other guys. And BB is our friend. Who really cares about everyone else? I don't know any of their names, where they live, what they like. And they don't really care about you and me. Anyone could eat the worm and they would be happy." I stood up and dumped the cup onto the ground.

Graham smiled. "You're right, *hermano*. Let's go tell BB."

Back in the cabin, BB was still sitting on his bed. I went up to him.

"BB, there's no way I'm going to eat a worm," I said. "Who cares about impressing those other kids?"

A smile spread across BB's face as he jumped up from his bunk. "I knew you guys were cool from the minute we first met," he said.

"Let's go to dinner," Tiny said. I felt like a huge weight had been lifted from my shoulders. I didn't know what I was going to tell everyone, but I was sure I'd think of something.

As soon as we walked through the door of the

dining hall, people started chanting "Raymond, Raymond!" I smiled and gave them a little wave.

"What are we going to do?" I asked Graham.

"Don't worry," he whispered. "Maybe they'll forget by the time dinner's over. Or maybe the award ceremony will start right after dinner."

Unfortunately, after each bite of my dinner, kids would come by to wish me good luck or slap me on the back and tell me how excited they were about the worm.

"I'm really sorry," BB said. "I guess you should do it if you really have to."

"No way," I replied. "It's not worth it, *hermano*." It suddenly hit me that this was the first time I had ever called anyone *hermano* besides Graham. And it had come out so easily. I was beginning to realize what good friends BB and Tiny had become to me and Graham.

As dinner ended, the pressure grew even more intense. Mark Herron's friend made his announcement that Mark was about to begin, but everyone started chanting my name instead.

"This is bad, Graham. What are we going to do?" All of a sudden BB got up and ran out the door without even cleaning up his tray.

"Where's he going?" Graham asked.

"I don't know. I think he just feels bad. You know, like he's responsible for me not going through with this." Graham and I still didn't know what we were going to tell everyone. We looked on as Mark made his most disgusting creation yet. As soon as he swallowed, the crowd immediately turned to me. The chanting became louder and louder. Finally, Graham stood up on the bench.

"I know you have all been waiting for Raging Raymond's dessert. But we've had a technical difficulty. We searched and searched, but we couldn't find a worm." Silence struck the lodge and everyone just stared at us. The silence was followed by a few boos, which were followed by a million boos. I was about to make a run for our cabin when BB showed back up with a cup.

"Hold on, everyone. I've got Raging Raymond's dessert right here!" BB said. He held up a cupful of dirt and made his way through the crowd. Everyone cheered and made a path for him up to me.

"Dude, way to build the suspense," Mark said.

Graham put his hand to my ear and whispered, "What is he doing?"

I shrugged my shoulders and leaned down to BB. "What are you doing?"

"Just trust me." Then he dug his fingers into the dirt. "I present Raging Raymond with his Spoonful of Doom!" He pulled out a long worm covered in dirt.

"You don't have to do this, BB," I told him. By now I felt like I could live with everyone being mad at me. I really didn't want to eat the worm.

I took the worm from BB and held it up by one end. I started to wipe off the dirt, but BB stopped me.

"Eat it with the dirt." Now I was really going to be sick. Eating a worm is bad enough, but did I have to eat a bunch of dirt too? The worm felt strange and not very slimy. I looked closer at the spot where I had wiped off the dirt. BB hadn't given me a real worm at all—it was one of his gummy worms covered in dirt!

"Looks delicious." I opened my mouth and dangled the worm over it. The crowd cheered as I slowly lowered it into my mouth and began to chew. The dirt tasted terrible, but luckily there was a lot more gummy worm than there was dirt. I made a big show of swallowing it, and everyone screamed and cheered.

I took a bow and it was over. Graham and BB took bows too. The crowd was going wild.

"Sorry about the dirt, but it helped hide the gummy worm," BB whispered to me.

As campers finished eating they moved outside for the awards ceremony. It was time to pay up on our bet. Suddenly, the glory of the worm eating didn't seem to matter. We headed back to our cabins with all the other Toad Claws to get our hats.

We rummaged through our bags looking for clean underwear. Then we all met up outside and waited for Toad. We stood there quietly, each of us with a pair of underpants in our hands. We didn't want to put them on our heads until the very last moment. After a while Toad came jogging down the path.

He made his way to the middle of our group and said, "Well, Toad Claws, since it was my fault for getting you into this mess, I'll be the first to put my hat on." He pulled his waistband open and stretched his underpants over his head until they fit snugly. They were blue. Toad looked hilarious, and we couldn't help cracking up.

"No, Toad, I think it was my fault for agreeing to this part of the bet," Tiny said, putting his underpants on his head. He didn't even need to stretch them to put them on. They were so big and loose that they fell down over his eyes. Now we really busted up laughing. Tiny walked around with his underpants covering his eyes and his arms stretched out in front of him like he was blindfolded.

"My turn," Carl said. He giggled as he pulled his pair over his head. They had rocket ships on them, and there was a big hole that his ear stuck out of. Graham laughed so hard he fell on the ground. I felt like my sides were going to split open. The rest of us happily pulled our underpants hats on. Some were boxers; others were tighty whities; some had holes in them like Carl's; and some, like Lizzy-Boy's, looked like they might have been worn already. We couldn't stop laughing.

"Okay, Toad Claws, it's time for our march of shame," Toad announced. He stepped up onto a bench. "The awards ceremony is about to start. I want you guys to follow me, because we're going to make a huge scene when we get there. If we have to wear underpants on our heads, we're going to make the most of it! Who's with me?"

"We are!" we screamed.

"Then let's go! Follow me!"

We proudly made our way down to the lodge, where everyone had already gathered for the ceremony. Toad made up a song as we marched. He would sing a line and then we would repeat it back to him.

"I don't know, but I've been told," he sang.

And we all repeated: "I don't know, but I've been told . . ."

". . . Toad Claws did not win the gold!"

". . . Toad Claws did not win the gold," we echoed.

"But what we have to do instead . . ."

"But what we have to do instead . . ."

". . . is wear our underpants on our heads!"

". . . is wear our underpants on our heads!"

We kept singing it over and over as we walked into the lodge. At first everyone was pointing and laughing at us. Then as we continued singing, some of the other groups joined in and sang along, clapping in unison. Toad marched us right to the front where Fuzzy was standing. After one more verse, Toad motioned for us to stop singing, and we took a bow. The crowd roared. Even Fuzzy was clapping. We all sat down.

"Thank you for sneaking in so quietly," Fuzzy joked. Then he began the awards ceremony.

Whenever one of the Muscular Monsters won an award, he would accept the medal from Fuzzy and then turn to the crowd and flex his muscles. Everyone would cheer. When BB won the gold for the swimming event, he walked up, accepted his

medal, turned his puny body toward the audience, and flexed his tiny muscles. The crowd went crazy. Tiny accepted his award for the rope climb and gave a friendly wave to the cheering audience.

"Now for the overall Olympic gold medal," Fuzzy announced. "This is for the team with the highest combined point total." Even before he announced their names, Flex was heading for the front.

"Muscular Monsters are the best!" David shouted to the crowd, as Flex accepted the gold medal. There were a few cheers and a handful of boos. I guess David had made a few new enemies at camp.

Fuzzy held his hand up for silence. "I consider our final award to be the most important. You've all spent the last few days together with boys you've met for the first time. You've worked together, had fun together, and become a bear patrol together. The Spirit Award is for the patrol that most clearly demonstrates the spirit of Camp Grizzly."

One by one Fuzzy asked each patrol to give their cheer again. When it was our turn I hopped around as I held up my finger and shouted, "Har! Toad Claws!" Even though I figured we probably wouldn't win, I felt my own Grizzly pride for my patrol. The Muscular Monsters laughed at us again. But this time I didn't care.

Fuzzy held up twelve leather necklaces with a golden bear claw hanging from each of them. "This was a difficult decision, but this year's award goes to . . ." He paused. "Wait, did I ever tell you the story about the time when I was a camper? Maybe we should wait until later for the award— this is a good story."

Everyone shouted, "No!"

"Just kidding, Grizzlies." Fuzzy laughed. "This year's Camp Grizzly Spirit Award goes to . . . THE TOAD CLAWS!"

We had won! We went crazy, hopping up and down, screaming and cheering. We proudly hopped to the front of the lodge, still wearing our underpants on our heads. Everyone was cheering except the Muscular Monsters. They were looking at each other and shaking their heads. We lined up, and Fuzzy hung a golden bear claw around each of our necks.

Graham, Tiny, BB, and I all high-fived each other over and over again.

Later that night we had our final Roses, Thorns, and Buds. Toad went first.

"Well, Toad Claws, I don't know what to say. My rose is each of you guys. You made me proud to be a Toad Claw today. I hope you will always re-member: if you can be a winner wearing a pair of underpants on your head, you can do anything." We all clapped, and Toad sat down.

BB stood up and was quiet for about a minute. "You guys have been awesome. None of you have made fun of me for liking bugs, or Graham for pretending he has a girlfriend, or Carl for picking his nose—"

"What? I don't pick my nose!" Carl interrupted. We all giggled.

"I guess I just want to say thanks. It's been a great time." Then BB threw his fists into the air and yelled, "Toad Claws *rule!*"

Tiny got up next. He had his usual smile on his face. "This has been the best week of my life. I've learned so much. Not just about hiking and swimming and other camp stuff, but I learned that I really shouldn't jump off the top bunk when someone's foot is close by. I learned that I can throw toilet paper really far. And best of all, I learned that I look great with underwear on my head." We clapped, and Tiny sat down.

Graham stood up next. His gold claw clinked against the big bear claw with the China sticker on it. I guess now he's two parts bear.

"Toad is the best, you guys are the best, Camp Grizzly is the best!" Graham said. "Oh, and did I ever tell you about my girlfriend, Kelly? Because she's the best too." We all busted up.

It was finally my turn.

"I never thought I'd say this, but hopping around like a pirate toad with my claw in the air is the cool-

est thing I've ever done. HAR! TOAD CLAWS!"
When I hopped around, everyone joined in.

I thought we'd never go to sleep that night. We
went to bed but stayed awake for hours just talking and laughing. All of a sudden it was morning
and Toad was singing us one last wake-up song.
We all packed up and headed for the lodge.

When we got to the lodge, I saw that my mom
was already there with a bunch of other parents. We introduced each other to our parents
and showed them our Spirit Award bear claws.
Just as Graham and I were about to leave, Tiny
said, "Wait, guys! I've got something for you."
He reached into his bag and handed each of us a
piece of paper. It was three copies of a picture he
had drawn of all four of us—me, BB, Tiny, and
Graham. In his picture we were all sitting on the
bench in front of the cabin. Our fingers were all
shaped like claws, and on each of our heads was,
you guessed it, a pair of underpants.

"You drew a picture for your friends? How
sweet!" Mom said. She squinted her eyes and

looked closer. "Are those *underpants* on your heads?" she asked.

We all cracked up at that.

"I have something for you guys too," BB said. He handed a little folded piece of paper to Graham and then one to me.

"You can open them later," he said. He seemed kind of shy all of a sudden.

"Come on, boys. It's time to go," Mom reminded us. We did our Toad Claw cheer one last time and said our good-byes.

As soon as we got into the car, Graham and I unfolded our pieces of paper from BB. Mine simply said WORM MAN. I showed it to Graham.

"What's yours say?" I asked him.

"THE TP KING," he said, showing it to me. "I guess we finally got some nicknames."

I tried it out. "Hmm, Worm Man." I wasn't sure if I really wanted to replace Raymond with Worm Man, but it still felt pretty cool to have my own nickname.

On the ride home Graham and I told my mom

about everything we'd done that week: the hiking, the swimming, and almost everything else. We didn't tell her about stealing David's underpants.

"Speaking of swimming," Mom said. "I was talking to Brad's mother this morning, and when I told her I was picking you up today, she invited you to their pool party later. She said she would have invited you earlier, but she thought you weren't getting back from camp until tomorrow."

"Really?" I asked. I thought about how much fun it would be to see everybody and tell them all about BB's bugs, Tiny's amazing toilet paper throw, and how we'd paraded around with underpants on our heads. Somehow, though, I just didn't think they would understand.

"So do you want to go to the party together?" Graham asked.

"Nah, I'm not really in the mood," I said. "But it's nice to be invited."